UNDER THE BIG MONTANA SKY

Jillian Carole

authorHOUSE®

AuthorHouse™
1663 Liberty Drive, Suite 200
Bloomington, IN 47403
www.authorhouse.com
Phone: 1-800-839-8640

© 2007 Jillian Carole. All rights reserved.

No part of this book may be reproduced, stored in a retrieval system, or transmitted by any means without the written permission of the author.

First published by AuthorHouse 11/28/2007

ISBN: 978-1-4343-3836-5 (sc)

Printed in the United States of America
Bloomington, Indiana

This book is printed on acid-free paper.

I dedicate this book to my family and friends who helped me to make it a reality.

Chapter 1

"I can't believe that you have sent this money hungry artist friend of yours a round trip ticket up here!" Jo said through clenched teeth to her mother.

"Now Jo, you are over reacting by a country mile. Sarah has no idea how much money I have. She doesn't have a clue. I have never found a way to bring it up in casual conversation and she has never brought it up either. I think it's going to be quite a shock to her really, when she gets here." Alice added, blue eyes flashing annoyance at her daughter's assumption about Sarah. "And another thing," she added shaking a finger up at Jo who towered over her 5'2" frame, "I expect you to be on your best behavior. Sarah is my friend, and I don't have that many people I call friend."

Jo shook her head in exasperation "She is only after that trust fund you set up for her. Was that her idea? I bet it was"

Alice scowled at her daughter, "You have the worst opinion of people. For your information Sarah doesn't even know that trust fund exists, and she won't either until I am dead and buried, unless you say something stupid so keep your mouth shut about that. It is nothing she needs to know about right now. It would only make her feel awkward."

Jo snorted, "Awkward? You have set enough aside that she will never really have to work again and you think she will feel awkward?" the vein on Jo's forehead was throbbing frustration. "I think she will try to knock you off as fast as she can. That's what I think. How can you be so gullible?"

Alice shook her head and put her hand up, "I will not hear another word from you on this topic. I have made my decision. It is still my ranch and I still decide what happens on it. If you can't be civil than why not stay in your cabin and hibernate the whole time she is here, like you are so good at doing." Jo's eyes took on a pained expression and Alice realized that she had hit a nerve too hard and she stopped and changed tone "I'm sorry Jo, I didn't mean anything by that last remark. It was just mean spirited of me. I was being cruel because I feel like you are attacking my friend before you even meet her. Who knows, you might like her, she is just a few years younger then you."

Jo sighed with resignation knowing that arguing with her mother was a waste of time and effort. She had yet to win one argument and often wondered why she still bothered at all. "Well, you are going to do what you are going to do, but don't expect me to roll out the red carpet for this Sarah woman."

Alice sighed and glancing at her watch said "Oh, I have to go, if I am going to make it to the airport before she does."

Chapter 2

Shifting restlessly in her economy plane seat, Sarah wished for the hundredth time that she had, at least, specified a window seat. "This is going to be a long flight" she thought to herself twirling a piece of her long chestnut brown hair around a strong, slender finger. Her pleasant features and soft mouth were pushed into an unconsciously alluring pout while she silently berated herself. She was very good at self-berating.

"At least you could have brought something to read...Where is your brain today? Obviously you left it somewhere else... maybe hanging on the hook in the bathroom." She continued to mentally fuss at herself, knowing full well that the real reason for her ongoing grumbling was the ball of butterflied excitement building in the pit of her stomach. She was finally going to meet Alice. Alice Thompson, her friend and mentor of nearly five years.

She happily thought back to the day when they first met each other. Sarah had just ended a messy relationship with a messy breakup, swearing never to do that again. She began to build a life as a single person, finding a feeling of wholeness that she did not expect. Shortly after her break up, she began inspecting the

Internet as a fun and safe place to interact socially with no serious consequences. After all if someone stepped on her toes she just went to another chat room. After surfing through many chat rooms, and finding mostly thoughtless banter or descriptions of sex acts that made her ears burn red, she had settled into a world events chat room, where the guided discussions were closely monitored and sex talk was strictly forbidden. Sarah had been visiting this room for several weeks and had participated in a few discussions, occasionally even heatedly, when Alice dropped in. After an evening of defending a woman's right to have a mind of her own and having back up in the room, Sarah invited Alice to chat privately, Alice agreed and the two of them switched to private chat to discuss women's issues with each other. After nearly the entire night had slipped by, Sarah realized joyfully she had discovered a like-minded woman, someone who was as wildly liberal and conservative at the same time and in the same ways as she was. She had finally found someone who she could respect and look up to. Right then and there she asked Alice to vow friendship and to meet her back in the world events chat room the next week. Alice had agreed and over the next five years their friendship had matured into a deep sharing of life events.

Unlike Sarah's own timid mother who had been through six failed marriages, Alice, at 78, had lived her life head on. It had been a very full and exciting life, doing everything she had ever dreamed of and more, all the while married to the same good-hearted man. Since Alice's husband died seven years before Sarah had met her, Alice had also been learning to live the life of a single and happy woman. Content to be one and whole instead of half of a pair, much to the astonishment of her friends and daughter who seemed to feel that she should be happier married.

Sarah was so pleased with the friendship that had developed between herself and this extraordinary lady. She felt honored and a bit intimidated to have this great woman's interest. With Alice's encouragement, Sarah had begun to take more chances and really live her life. Of course, this had not set well with her friends who were used to her the way she had always been. The few men who had tried unsuccessfully to settle her down and reform her into a good wife, gave up after a while and drifted away.

Sarah reasoned with herself "Maybe, I'm just an untamable spirit." she thought shaking her mane of hair, "Why should I give anything up for a man that I feel no connection with...no magic...there should be magic... electricity...fire...yet all I feel at the strongest...is perhaps, a friendly affection." she frowned "Maybe I will find my soul mate yet. I just haven't found the right person. Someday I will meet someone that understands me, and won't crowd me or suffocate me but instead will encourage me and leave me alone when I need my creative space. I would be willing to do the same thing."

She shifted on to happier thoughts. Admittedly her life was a whole lot more fun and spontaneous and her artwork really reflected the shift her life view had taken. Her career as an artist was finally on it's way, she smiled thinking, "imagine all but three pieces selling at my last show. Unheard of!" and she had several respected galleries vying for her to show her work there too. Then there was that commissioned piece that she had been asked to do. Returning to the reality of the cramped, hard seat she was sitting in, she wished again that she had upgraded to a business class ticket, knowing that she could have been able to afford it. "Really you can afford it now." she said aloud thumping her fist lightly on the arm rest, much to the surprise of the passenger next to her. Eyebrows raised, he glanced at her over his paper trying to determine if she was talking and thumping at him.

To hide her embarrassment, she began to dig around in her bag for her sketch pad and one of her artist pencils. Vowing to herself that on the way home she would upgrade and fly business class, she pulled out a brand new sketch pad, a pencil and eraser. Her last pad was almost used up and the cover had fallen off somewhere along the way so she had dashed out and grabbed a new one just before leaving Houston on this trip. Such a hot smoggy place, "Someday I will move away from there and never go back, except to visit friends or maybe for an art show." she thought to herself as she gently struggled the plastic off and flipped the clean cover open. Anticipation overtook her, wiping all other thoughts from her mind as it did every time she looked at a blank sheet of paper or a clean blank canvas.

"What are you going to be?" she asked the blank sheet quietly.

She raised her stunning emerald green eyes and searched the cramped cabin for something interesting to draw. Her gaze landed on a beautiful slender Asian woman with long black hair and perfect skin. She looked her over slowly, deeply appreciating her beautiful lines. Her eyes undressed the woman's austere curves referencing countless life models from her past. Allowing her gaze to slide up to the woman's face she found widened dark almond eyes looking back at her uncomfortably. "Maybe not." she said quietly to herself. She continued to browse the many bodies available to her, an attitude learned from drawing countless nude models. Then her gaze fell on a small child that was hanging out of a seat several rows ahead of her boldly staring back at her with open curiosity. Without thought she began drawing the child as quickly as she could. The impish curiosity and the blond silky hair flying everywhere, entranced Sarah, as well as the impossible positions held momentarily. Now hanging up side down, with her dress up to her bellybutton, over the arm rest, now a quick dash into the aisle to look around, now a half face, frozen over the back of the seat, her large blue eyes watching Sarah the whole time. After what seemed only a moment the seat belt warning signs came on and the speaker said something about starting the decent.

Sarah quickly looked through her accumulation of sketches and selected one that she thought was fairly good, and signed it. Then she went up the aisle and gave it to the child's mother who had sat next to her the whole time quietly saying things like "Jamie sit up and hold still...please stop that...just look at your hair...what will Nana think if we get there and you are all a mess?" Sarah suspected by Jamie's lack of compliance and her mother's lack of enthusiasm that her mother probably said things like that all of the time and Jamie routinely ignored her. Jamie's mother was delighted with the drawing and thanked Sarah again and again until a scowling flight attendant told Sarah impatiently "Please return to your seat, we are about to land and you must be seated."

Once the plane landed it seemed as if she could not get off of it fast enough. Other passengers were blocking the aisle, rummaging for small packages in the overhead compartments. Sarah had only one thought running laps around her head. Alice's last email had said "I'll be wearing a red cowboy hat so you can spot me. Now Sarah, it's up to you because I don't know what you look like. I can't wait for you to introduce yourself." Sarah was almost weak kneed, but she took several quick deep breaths and plunged through the throng of people and off of the plane.

When they had agreed not to exchange photos ever, over the Internet or by mail, Sarah had not considered the possibility that they would actually meet in person. They had exchanged Christmas cards every year as well as Birthday cards and just because cards, but never a photo. Living on opposite sides of the country, Sarah had just not seriously considered it until Alice had mailed her a round trip ticket and invitation to come and see her spread. "I hope I brought enough clothes for Montana." Sarah thought to herself nervously "Surely it can't be cold up here all of the time. After all it is late spring." Trying to avoid her growing excitement, she thought back to the 90 degree temperatures that they had been having in Houston and how good cool weather would feel after the heat and humidity. Down the ramp in a jostle of people into a big crowd of waiting welcomes, the passengers came loping and bumping out of the plane. Suddenly in front of her, there was a huge red cowboy hat blocking her forward progress.

"Alice? Alice Thompson is that really you?" Sarah asked staring in uncertain joy at a wiry, deeply tanned woman with sparkling lively eyes peering out from under the largest red cowboy hat that Sarah had ever seen.

"Well, hell last time I looked in the mirror I was me! You must be Sarah then. It really is great to meet you in the flesh and blood after all of these years!" Alice replied flashing a big smile and pulling Sarah into a tight brief hug. Alice held Sarah out at arms length in a grip of steel. "You are beautiful child, simply beautiful...if only my Jo had your looks...Ah, well can't be helped, that one." Alice said, almost to herself.

Sarah was at a loss for words. She knew that Alice's daughter was a sore spot for Alice and they had rarely talked about her, sticking mostly to political topics and art trends. But Sarah had gathered that Jo was not your typical woman. Not having a reply to Alice's last comment, she frowned uncomfortably and then looked at the spry little old lady in that amazing great big red cowboy hat. She smiled and than began laughing. They both laughed for a while and finally between gasps Sarah said "Well, Alice, I sure didn't have any trouble finding you with that huge hat on. Where on earth did you find that?"

Alice herself near tears from laughing took a while to catch her breath before responding "I won it fair and square in a contest of wits from a fellow over in Billings. He swears it's the largest red cowboy hat in the world. I won it from him in a poker game years ago, but I don't believe it would win any world records." She pulled the hat off of her head revealing short straight silver hair and held it out in front of her "But it sure does attract attention!" And she threw her head back and let out a loud whoop of laughter. Sarah looked around self-consciously but no one paid them much attention. Everyone was too busy saying their own hellos.

"Well let's grab your bags and get home. It's a long drive from here." Alice motioned her down in the direction of the baggage claim area and off they went. In no time they were in Alice's new barn red Dodge dually truck headed out of town on a two lane highway and laughing all of the way. The wild red cowboy hat softly thudded against the back of Alice's seat, keeping tempo with the road. After about forty minutes they turned off the highway onto a small paved private road that led up to a group of buildings in the distance.

As they approached Alice began apologizing to Sarah "Now I know you had no idea how wealthy I really am because I sort of didn't mention it and you don't run in ranching circles, but please, dammit, don't get all weird on me now…I am just normal folk…we've been talking for years…I am still just me."

Sarah had no idea what Alice was talking about until they finally drove into the small group of houses, stables and assorted buildings scattered about the complex that she had thought was a small town and she realized that all of these buildings were Alice's. All of the property that they had been driving on was Alice's too. Alice's spread was huge.

Sarah didn't say anything for a moment, instead she allowed herself time to absorb this new little bit of information. "Well," she finally thought to herself "She's right. She is the exact same person she was a minute ago when we were laughing and joking." Sarah still felt a bit overwhelmed.

Alice pulled to a stop in front of the biggest house in the group. Sarah could only wonder at the size of the main house. It was two or maybe three stories and shaped in a fort like square with a porch that doubled as a deck for the upstairs rooms that went all the way around the house, as best as Sarah could tell. She immediately loved the place. The long porch swing invited her to sit for hours and swing the afternoon away in the shade. With a start Sarah noticed a tree sticking out of the middle of the house and realized "There must be a garden there that the house wraps around. What a wonderful place." Dark barn red with clean, white window frames that the house seem all the more imposing, solid, and heavy. Sarah thought, "I would paint this house a pale yellow and leave the white around the windows or maybe a pale pumpkin. Pumpkin would be nice."

Alice looked over at her passenger, her clear blue eyes searching Sarah's face for her reaction to the shear size of her spread, afraid she might find her intimidated beyond friendship, "Well here we are." she piped in nervously "This is the main house. More like a command post if you ask me." She crinkled her face up. In concern she watched as Sarah took it all in. Knowing that she had lost a few friends in this moment, having them become overwhelmed by her wealth to the point of alienation and hoping Sarah would not be another one, she sighed, then went on with determination, "Everyone out." Alice was out the door and halfway to the house yelling "SAM…SAM…Where are you Sam? Get out here and unload these bags for me. I've already helped to carry them once today, that's enough for these old bones."

A young lanky fellow, perhaps twenty, came flying out from between two buildings, tripped, got up and hurried up to the truck. Dusting himself off he said, "Sorry to keep you Mrs. Thompson, Sam is busy I'll be glad to get those for you." All the time he was speaking, he watched Sarah with curiosity. "Where would you like me to put them ma'am?" he asked as he grabbed up the bags out of the back of the pickup.

"Oh, Lucas, just put them in that nice room next to mine would you?" Alice replied in a motherly tone as she walked towards the house.

Sarah followed behind, trying to soak in as much as she could, never had she been to a place with so many wonderful views and such interesting possibilities. "If only I had brought my paint box and traveling easel," she thought to herself wistfully, then pulling herself back to the moment, she tried to catch up with her host. Alice who was eyeing her from the worn gray planks of the porch with uncertain concern.

"I know I should have told you how wealthy I am so you wouldn't be so shocked." Alice said frowning misinterpreting Sarah's hesitation "but it just never came up and after a while I didn't know how to bring it up. You know, oh by the way I'm really well off just sounded so crazy." Alice closely inspected Sarah who was once again looking off. She abruptly stopped talking, realizing that her first instinct had been right and Sarah was nearly oblivious to the wealth, "Poor child only has eyes for the pictures she could paint. She'd rather starve and paint than not paint. Thank goodness her paintings are selling so well right now."

Sarah was in her own world, the world of an artist. All she saw was the gentle colors of the small pale green spring leaves shivering on the dark imposing trees around the complex. She thought to herself "that kind of leaf lasts all of a day in Houston. Ah, to have the time to paint those leaves as they slowly unfold themselves. Just to watch them unfold would be wonderful... and this rolling Montana land... incredible."

Alice thought while waiting for Sarah to make it up the stairs "I'm glad I set up that trust fund for her last year. Nothing she needs to know about until the time comes." Aloud Alice said, "Watch out for those steps they are taller then you would think."

Immediately Sarah came back to the present. Glancing around, she realized that both Lucas' polite brown eyes and Alice's dancing blue eyes were watching her while they stood on the porch waiting for her. She immediately began apologizing as she hurried up the steps "I'm so sorry, I didn't mean to keep you both, but it is so lovely here and so different from Houston. It's just beautiful. I didn't mean for you'all to wait for me. Oh..." her voice trailed off, her hands fluttering down to her sides as they walked into the main entrance to the house and up the gently curving staircase. Across a walkway that overlooked the entrance on one side, she followed her elegant host and the clomping dusty Lucas into a hall.

"Here you go Sarah. This will be your room while you're here." Alice said pointing to a beautiful paneled white door with an old-fashioned glass doorknob. Sarah opened the door and a grateful Lucas headed into the room and unceremoniously dropped her luggage at the foot of the bed on a blanket chest and headed back out with a slight nod of his head "Ma'am".

Alice continued without noticing the interruption "Mine's next door, right there" She said indicating a similar door further down the hall. "Feel free to bug me any time. Now why don't you freshen up and take a rest or wander around the grounds. I have a little business to attend to, I hope you don't mind, but I am going to have to leave you to your own devises for a little while. Dinner's in a coupla' hours at 6 PM sharp. The dress is very casual but everyone who is here is expected to come and be on time. I'll see you then. If you need anything press the button next to the door here" Alice said pointing out the small lit button, "and someone from the house staff will come, and I'll see you for dinner, bye now dear." Alice paused at the door and added, "I'm so glad you decided to come."

Sarah watched Alice bustle off back down the hall they had just come up and head off down the stairs somewhere, then she turned and walked into her room for the next few weeks. It was really quite large for a guest room and it had several doors leading off of it. The combination of a rainbow of soft colors gently vibrated around the room inviting Sarah in as if the room had been custom ordered just for her. French doors led out onto the deck she had noticed earlier facing the front of the house but what really caught her eye was what lay on the other side of one of those open doors. It was a bathroom as big as her living room back home, with a sunken pale turquoise marble whirl pool in the middle of the floor that she thought she could probably swim in. Kicking her shoes off, and sinking her toes into the matching soft pale turquoise carpet, she quickly inspected the rest of the room and decided that she would spend some time unpacking and then maybe go exploring a little bit before dinner. After getting her clothes and accessories stored away in the walk in closet, it had both shelves and hangers, located in the bathroom area, and her toiletries set out by the sink where there was a wide space and a stool, Sarah sat down on the bed only to discover that it was as soft as could be. "Well maybe I'll just rest here for a minute" she thought snuggling down into what had to be a down mattress topper. "Oh, I have got to get one of these." she thought to herself blissfully as she instantly dozed off.

A soft rapping on the door woke Sarah. Reorienting herself to where she was she called out "Come in."

The door opened wide and a short round woman with dark eyes and hair walked in. "Dinner will be in fifteen minutes. I thought I would wake you so you would have a few minutes before the dinner bell rang. In the future when you decide to take a nap, you might want to set the alarm clock next to the bed there, dear." she said with a laughing tone in her gentle voice. "Alice takes dinner very seriously. You would not want to be late." Her voice was cheerful, melodious and in no way rude as she bustled around the room fluffing and picking imaginary lint off of things. "My name's Maria, and if you need anything just let me know. I'm chief cook and bottle washer around this joint." she chuckled at her own funny and was gone, softly shutting the door behind her, before Sarah had a chance to say one word.

Sarah blinked trying to fit this bit of information into her still waking brain. Abruptly she was awake, "fifteen minutes until dinner" she thought in instant clarity. Up she jumped and into the bathroom she dashed. She quickly brushed her hair while looking herself over in the mirror. "I look thin, tired and my eyes are puffy" she sighed, "and the only thing I can do is change clothes into something less rumpled and more comfortable. I can't believe I dozed off in panty hose." Off came the hated knee high panty hose landing almost on top of the shoes she had discarded earlier. Next to hit the floor were the camel colored slacks, thin brown leather belt still in the belt loops, now hopelessly wrinkled. The soft cream silk blouse finished out the small heap on the floor. "The best resale clothes I own in a pile on the floor" she sighed. Into the closet she dashed. Emerging moments later in a pair of soft, faded jeans and a loose pullover sweater almost the same pale turquoise as the carpet, she was glad that she had brought her comfortable clothes along. She slipped into a pair of warm socks and crocks and, deciding to leave her hair loose, headed down stairs just in time to hear the dinner bell ring.

Upon reaching the bottom of the stairs, she stopped in the two and a half story front foyer, with four possible choices not counting the stairs she had just come down, two halls leading off in opposite directions one off to the east and one off to the west, an arched doorway and a short hall that lead off to the south under the stairs and ended in what looked like French doors to the outside, and waited for some indication of where dinner might be in this large rambling house. Hearing voices off to her right, she followed the sounds, walking through a large arched doorway she found herself in what looked like an executive's office right down to the leather sofa against one wall. Alice looked up from the desk where she was reading over some paperwork as Sarah came in. Standing in front of the desk was a small man who looked like he was made of bones and whipcord with a haggard expression on his face. He had on jeans, boots, and a flannel shirt and was dusty from head to toe. He stopped mid sentence and turned to look at her from where he stood. Sarah could tell from his gaze that he was sizing her up and wondered curiously what he saw. Alice smiled a big smile, immediately making Sarah feel welcome and said. "Hi, we're almost done here. Why don't you come on in? Sarah, this is Sam. Sam this is Sarah. She's from Houston, up for a visit."

Sarah smiled hesitantly and said "I heard the dinner bell, but can't find dinner." she shrugged.

Alice burst out laughing and Sam joined in. Sarah laughed too and Alice said between chuckles "Well, why don't we head over there right now? What do you say Sam? Think this can wait?"

"Sure, Alice this stuff isn't anywhere near as important as dinner." Sam said chuckling and shaking his head.

"Oh you hush, you old goat." Alice replied to his friendly jab as she rose from her chair and walked around the desk. Sarah noticed a slight fatigue in her friends face and then it was gone, masked behind her joking, sparkly eyes. They all walked out of the office and through the main entrance area, towards the back of the room, past the stairs it ended in a set of French doors like the ones in her room. But instead of going through the doors, they turned left and headed down a hall that must have been directly under the hall upstairs. Sarah could see that several large rooms opened out onto this hall from both sides. One they passed looked like an old fashioned library and the next one had a long intricately carved table running down the middle of it. "This must be the dinning room," thought Sarah. She almost ran into Alice, as she went to turn into the room, because Alice kept going straight.

Alice glanced at her and smiled "Oh that old room is the formal dining room. We hardly ever use it, just wasted space as far as I'm concerned. To big to talk in and expect anyone to hear you right. We're going around the corner" She said as she pointed down the hall vaguely, "to the regular dining room on the east wing where everything happens. It's really the heart of this house." Without another word they turned a corner and went all the way down the hall. At the end of the hall a wonderful room opened before them with a long table made out of a single piece of wood that must have come from an immense tree. There were two long benches that ran along each side of the table made out of the same heavy wood construction. "It must be some kind of pine." Sarah guessed. The floor was a Mexican terra cotta tile covered here and there with beautiful woven Indian rugs. The room's dimensions were vast running the whole width of the east wing, with floor to ceiling windows on two sides that looked out at a formal garden to the west and south to the countryside beyond. At the east end of the room there was a massive stone fireplace that glowed with the warmth of burning logs and had a grouping of inviting chairs around it. Sarah understood immediately why this would be the room of choice with its breathtaking panoramic view and snug corners obviously set up for after dinner discussion. It was almost like being outside.

Maria bustled in from a door to the right of the entrance and announced dinner with a quiet little bell. Everyone sat down. Sarah only then noticed how many people were assembled. "There must be nearly twenty people here," she thought to herself realizing that most were hard-handed men in dusty work clothes, though there were a few tough looking women in the group. She, Alice and Maria seemed to be the only people at the table who were not covered head to foot in dirt. Sarah also noticed that Maria sat down with everyone else at the table. The food began to be passed around and discussion picked up between mouthfuls about the day and how the branding and vaccination of the cattle was going. Laughter and joking was everywhere. A few curious glances were directed at Sarah, but she was almost immediately drawn into discussion by Sam who had quietly positioned himself to her right. Alice was way down at the end of the table joking along with the work-hands about how stinky they were. Playfully holding her nose and saying that she would have to position herself down wind tomorrow so she could eat her dinner in peace. This brought a large amount of chuckles and laughter from everyone as she pantomimed holding her breath and trying to eat. Maria, who sat immediately to Alice's left and closest to, what must have been the kitchen door, leaned over to Alice and said something that brought Alice's eye to rest on Sarah. Immediately everyone's attention turned to Sarah and the room quieted with anticipation.

The hair on the nap of Sarah's neck stood up as Alice, still chuckling, said in a loud voice "Sarah, Sarah stand up so everyone can get a good look at you, since everyone is trying to sneak peeks anyway. Come on, it's too late to be shy now."

Quietly Sarah made a half stand, the bench in the back of her knees making it impossible to stand all the way up and sort of waved at everyone. This brought a quiet chuckle from several individuals. "Hi." she said.

Everyone looked at each other and then immediately waved back and said "Hi" in one loud voice, making her turn pink to the roots of her hair. As she sat down, Alice said in a reproachful tone over the chuckles "Now, now this is my friend Sarah, you be nice to her. Just look what you've done. Your teasing has turned her all pink." To Alice's last comment everyone broke out in friendly laughter.

Sam patted her on the back and said quietly "They mean no harm Sarah, they are just welcoming you into the group trying to make you feel a part." Sarah smiled and hoped no one could tell what abject misery this was for her. All the while fervently wishing the attention would soon be diverted on to someone or something else.

Alice said in a more serious voice. "Sam I'm putting her under your care. You make sure that all of her questions are answered and she gets any help she may need when I'm not around to do the job myself."

"Yes, ma'am." Sam smiled reassuringly at Sarah. "Now don't you worry, you can ask me anything and I can answer it, as long as it is about this ranch."

Immediately the discussion and noise in the room returned, only to have Alice's voice rise once again above the general chaos "Where's Jo, dammit?" the noise of the room instantly died down as everyone stopped talking and a nervous silence fell over the group. "Sam, where is my wayward child now." someone coughed and there were a few shuffling feet.

Sam cleared his throat "Alice, now you know that Jo does what she wants. She is as strong minded a woman as you are." Everyone nervously chuckled to this. "Some would say she was even possibly a tad more stubborn then you if that's humanly possible."

Alice interrupted him "Sam get to the point...stop trying to make excuses for her."

"Yes ma'am" Sam sighed looking around the table for support, everyone was glancing here and there.

It was obvious that everyone in the room with the exception of herself and Alice knew exactly where Jo was and did not want to tell Alice. Sarah thought to herself with great curiosity "Everyone in this room has absolute loyalty to Jo, even over Alice. She must be something else again."

"Well, Sam. I am waiting." Alice said sounding angry "I specifically told her to be here so she could meet Sarah and off she goes without even telling me. So what in the world could have been more important then being here this time?"

Sam shifted uncomfortably, obviously trying to come up with a good answer. "Well, Alice, Doc. Peterson called earlier and asked her to come in to town to talk to him about something. She didn't tell me what it was about, but this was the only time he had open until Tuesday and she didn't want to wait that long. She said that she was going to stay in town for the night and that she would be back tomorrow sometime."

Alice scowled, and looked worried "Well, at least she could have told me she was going. I hope it isn't anything." She rubbed her temples and sighed the energy draining right out of her while Sarah watched and then Alice straightened her shoulders and seemed to brush it away. Conversation resumed cautiously and soon the noise level was as high as it had been.

Sam leaned over to Sarah and asked, "So are you enjoying your dinner?"

Sarah smiled at his attempt to draw her into conversation realizing how quiet she had been, "Yes, Sam, Maria is a wonderful cook."

He chuckled in reply "Maria is the house manager, without her around we would starve in our dirty clothes and the house would fall down around us while we starved. She does everything well."

Sarah tried to imagine everything that went into running a household this large and felt overwhelmed by the prospect of it "That must be an incredibly difficult job."

After a while Maria stood up and announced "coffee's on the buffet along with some cookies for dessert and when you're done don't forget to put all of your dishes in the sink," and she was off to somewhere else in the house.

Moments after that Alice stood and said "Well, I am just worn out. Sarah, you will have to excuse me this evening. Maybe we can spend some time visiting tomorrow. Sam, please keep Sarah entertained for me won't you?"

Sam nodded in her direction in acceptance of the request. And Alice walked off down the hall. Sarah saw Maria meet her halfway down the hall and begin talking to her quietly as they turned the corner out of sight.

Long after dinner was over and the dishes were cleared, Sarah stood by one of the windows looking west out at the garden and the old tree that stood in solitary splendor in the center of the courtyard. The moonlight from a nearly full moon blued the scene turning the leaves into silver shadows. She could see lit rooms all around in the house and wondered if everyone who had eaten dinner at this now empty table also slept in this house, perhaps on the west wing.

Turning to go she was confronted by Sam's fatherly presence, "I didn't realize you were in here." she said surprised by his silent approach.

"I didn't mean to startle you," he said flashing a smile in the dimness of the room. "I was just wondering what you were doing standing here in the dark all alone."

Sarah realized how odd she must seem, and replied quietly "The gardens are so beautiful in the moon light and I couldn't see them well enough with the lights on so I turned them off for a better view. I didn't think anyone would mind. I didn't mean to cause any trouble."

Sam smiled again "Sarah, you have been no trouble at all to anyone. I hope you have a wonderful stay here. Alice just thinks the world of you and it has given her renewed energy just having you around. So don't go worrying all of the time. We are all glad you are here." and with that he turned and walked out of the room leaving Sarah to ponder what he meant when he said 'Alice's renewed energy.' "She had seemed tired, was Alice sick?" she wondered and what was this daughter Jo like that she could command such loyalty. "She must be something else." Sarah sighed and walked back to her "princess room" as she had begun calling it to herself worn out by the long day and ready to take a shower and get the travel grit off of her skin and slide back into that incredibly soft bed.

Chapter 3

The next morning, Sarah awoke at 7:30 to her alarm clock. She dressed in her running clothes and went down stairs to see what was going on today, only to find the house empty as far as she could tell. Finding one of those service buttons in the dining room by the door she pressed it in hopes of Maria appearing and telling her where everyone was.

A short time later a slender young girl with Maria's dark hair and eyes appeared "I'm Rosa, can I help you?" she asked politely. Sarah's disappointment must have been clear because she added "If you are hungry, I can reheat something for you, though usually if you miss breakfast you are on your own around here. Come on into the kitchen and I'll scrounge something up for you."

Following the girl into the kitchen Sarah said "Thank you, I would love a cup of coffee, but will pass on breakfast for now." realizing with a start that this must be one of Maria's children. "Where is Alice today, do you know?" she asked in a hopeful tone.

"Oh she's still in bed. It's a ritual around here. All the hands come down to breakfast but Mrs. Thompson takes hers in bed and reads the paper, answers her mail and types on the computer before she comes down. Would you like your breakfast brought up to you too?" Rosa asked.

Sarah shook her head no, and decided that after her morning jog maybe she would go up and "bug" Alice for a minute before eating breakfast. Aloud she said "She has her computer in her room?"

To which Rosa replied, "Oh she has several computers and they are all connected to each other. There's even one in the stable office that Dad, I mean Sam, uses for ordering supplies and stuff."

This slip of tongue aroused Sarah's curiosity "Sam is your Dad?" she asked Rosa.

"Oh yes and Maria is my Mother." Rosa went on cheerfully without encouragement "and Lucas is my brother, he's home from college for the summer. I have seven brothers and sisters, but only three of us are on the ranch right now, me, Lucas and my little sister, Cassi, short for Cassandra." Rosa placed a hot cup of coffee in front of Sarah and said, "Here you go. When you're done please put your cup in the sink and ring if you need anything else."

Sarah called to her just before she disappeared around the corner "When is breakfast around here anyway?" thinking to herself "I must have just missed it."

"Oh," Rosa smiled "well if you want to join the hands they eat at 5:00 so they can get out and to it by sunrise."

Sarah blinked "5:00 a.m.?" she said out loud "Well, maybe I will have my breakfast in bed after all. What time does Alice have her breakfast?" she asked thinking it must be quite a bit later.

"She usually has hers brought around 5:15 or so. That way we have time to get breakfast under way down here first, then one of us runs breakfast up to her real quick."

Sarah looked surprised then, realizing that Rosa was waiting on a reply said "I'll just hunt my own breakfast when I get back from running for now, thanks Rosa." Rosa shrugged indifferently and was gone.

The coffee was wonderful and strong and Sarah lingered over it enjoying the large sunbeam silence of the room and the sight of the garden outside. Last night's dew glistened on every plant in the bright morning light, turning the garden into a magical fairyland. A noise behind her caught her attention and she turned to find Alice smiling at her.

"Rosa said you were looking for me," she said. "I know I haven't been much company since you came up here, but I have been busy with all sorts of details that only I can deal with. If Jo were around, she could handle most of these things but she's not." she grumped "Maybe this afternoon I can make it up to you by showing you around if you would like and we'll visit then."

Sarah smiled glad to have something to look forward to "Sure. That sounds wonderful Alice. I usually take a short morning run before breakfast just to get my blood flowing again after a night of sleep, but I'm still asleep when you'all eat breakfast. What time is lunch so I don't miss it too?"

"Oh, lunch is catch as catch can around here. Maria packs lunches for the hands and everyone else is on their own. Breakfast and supper are the big meals." Alice replied looking preoccupied. "Look I have to go, but we'll visit this afternoon, I promise." she said flashing Sarah a brief smile as she turned to leave the room. "I sure am sorry to leave you on your own so much. But it can't be avoided today. I am so sorry." and she was gone not waiting for a reply. Once again the room became silent but this time it felt lonely. So Sarah took her cup into the kitchen and left them in the sink as requested and headed out into the brilliant Montana morning.

After stretching against one of the trees in front of the main house under the friendly gaze of several cats and a large sandy colored dog lying under the swing on the porch, Sarah started off down the long road that led to the highway. After some thought she had decided that she would jog down to the highway and back every morning as her route, figuring that the gentle rolls of the land would give her more of a workout then the flat roads of Houston. After reaching the highway she turned and began back up the road. Consciously keeping her breath in rhythm with her steps, she felt her muscles work in concert. Sarah loved the exhilaration of running and ran every morning no matter what the conditions. She was almost back to the house when she heard the sound of a vehicle approaching her from behind.

Suddenly a loud horn was honking and a vehicle roared by, running her off of the road onto the narrow gravel shoulder. She regained her composure and kept her pace even though her heart felt like it would pound out of her chest. As she watched the back of the large black Dodge dually truck with a huge chrome bumper cow guard that had tried to run her down fly up and park in front of the main house. "How rude" she thought to herself "It's not like I was in the middle of the road, he had lots of room." She continued watching to see, who the jerk getting out of that truck would be. "Probably some short guy with a lot to prove." she thought with grim amusement. Much to Sarah's surprise, a tall, lean woman wearing old blue jeans that molded to her powerful legs, a white, tucked in T-shirt and a straw cowboy hat stepped out of the truck. Her tan, work hardened arms hung loosely at her sides ending in heavy work gloves that concealed her hands completely. The strength of her broad shoulders became apparent as she casually grabbed a large bag of feed and slung it over one shoulder. Then balancing the feed lightly, she turned and looked at Sarah. The steady gaze of her dark eyes missed nothing as it traveled unhurriedly down and then up Sarah's slender body, pausing briefly to watch her breasts moving against the fabric of her shirt as Sarah continued to jog. Sarah suddenly felt naked and as their eyes finally made contact the fifty yards between them evaporated. The impact of those smoldering eyes left Sarah breathless as she unconsciously slowed to a walk and then stopped.

Silently the two of them regarded each other across the distance for what felt to Sarah like an eternity before the driver abruptly turned and walked off toward the stables. As if released from a spell, Sarah shook her head, and wondered aloud "Who was that woman?" already knowing the answer. That had to be Jo. Realizing that she was standing in the road, Sarah began walking towards the porch and the swing, her mind whirling from the encounter. Abruptly Sarah decided not to mention the incident to Alice "She seems to have so much on her mind already" she reasoned with herself. So she stretched her muscles again and carefully stepping over the dog that hadn't noticeably moved, sat down on the porch swing. Only after she was seated and had been swinging quietly for a while did she realize that her heart was still pounding as if she had just run a marathon instead of just down to the mail box and back, a trip of no more then a mile.

"What is this all about?" she thought to herself, never before had she been so moved by another person, much less by a simple look from fifty yards away. "This trip has been harder on me than I thought." casting about for explanation she thought, "I must be worn out. I wonder what altitude we are at, maybe I'm having trouble with the altitude." she simply refused to admit to herself that Jo's fiery gaze could possibly be the cause of her pounding heart. Abruptly she got up and headed into the house, "Maybe I'm hungry." she thought as she walked back into the dining room for a light breakfast. After breakfast and another cup of that wonderful coffee, Sarah went upstairs to clean up and change into clothes for the day. She settled on a pair of jeans and a flannel shirt, feeling the cool more strongly then her host, she slid into a pair of old brown Justin boots, picked up her sketch book and headed back down stairs and out onto the porch. She had planned to sit on the swing and sketch but decided to sit in a nearby rocking chair and draw the lazy dog under the swing instead. As far as she could tell he still hadn't moved from the spot she had first seen him in except maybe to shift his head a little. With complete focus she began drawing the dog and then she filled in the background including the stables. Occasionally her mind would conjure up a vision of Jo and she would find herself daydreaming about what Jo would have said if she had confronted her about nearly running her over, but sometimes the vision was only of Jo getting out of the truck and grabbing that sack and turning those dark eyes on her again. Again and Again she felt Jo's eyes running over her body, her skin tickling like a soft breeze. Over the course of the few hours that she sat there, the scene played itself over and over endlessly in her mind until she had every nuance in place. Quietly giving in to herself she sketched Jo as she had looked next to her truck, her heart pounding as if she were a cornered cat about to get a bath. After a while her heart calming a bit, she flipped the page and tried to draw her closer and from a slightly different angle.

"Hey there," Alice said in a cheery voice surprised by the strong jump she got out of Sarah. She thought to herself "and the way she flipped that sketch pad closed you'd wonder just what she was drawing in there." Alice laughed and said aloud from her perch in a golf cart "I didn't mean to startle you there Sarah, but it's nearly 2:30 and if we are going to do the tour we need to get started." she patted the seat next to her. "Come on then."

"Of course, I had just gotten so involved with my drawing that I must have lost track of time completely." Sarah said holding her sketch pad in white knuckles and thinking to herself, "I am going mad. Drawing Alice's daughter again and again like that. There is something wrong with me. Maybe it isn't the altitude after all. How can I have such strong feelings for someone I don't even know? This is impossible." She struggled to hide her confusion from Alice's watchful eyes by quickly walking around the barn red golf cart with white trim that Alice was sitting in and sliding onto the seat next to her. "Well, this sure is a nice way to get around." She said aloud trying to sound casual admiring the little electric cart. It was painted to match the house.

"You ain't seen nothin' yet!" Alice said and she stomped on the floor peddle. The little golf cart started forward as Alice tried unsuccessfully to spin its tires on the pavement. "Wahoo!" Alice yelled and started laughing at Sarah who had dropped her sketch pad and was now trying to retrieve it from where it lay wedged on the floorboards.

Sarah laughed at herself too, realizing that she should take Sam's sage advice and worry less and have more fun. Lately she seemed to be taking life way too seriously again. "I think I saw your daughter come home." Sarah said trying to sound very casual.

"Big boned woman, black hair, probably in jeans and a white T-shirt?" Alice asked "All muscle head to foot?" Alice added "Not a ribbons and bows type of woman, and it's my fault for raising her out here on a ranch around all of these rough and tumble ranch hands. She's tough as nails though, and really good at running things." Sarah noticed the sadness in Alice's voice and realized that Jo was not what Alice had in mind when she first held her new baby girl in her arms. Alice had slowed the cart down to a crawl as they kept talking.

"She seems nice enough." Sarah said waving her hands vaguely and thinking about this morning. Suddenly Sarah asked "Is Jo her given name or is it short for something? It really seems to fit her."

"Oh no, it's not her given name but lord forbid if you call her by anything else. No her given name is Josephine. I had hoped that she would be tall and slender with a willowy grace and her daddy's black hair and dark eyes and that she would be married by now and making me beautiful grandbabies to hold and spoil." Alice sighed with obvious disappointment. "Well she got the eyes, hair and height, but none of the rest." Alice was shaking her head sadly "you know she is nearly 6 feet tall, right under it, she could have been a model if only she were graceful in a gentle way instead of like some kind of a mountain cat. Ah well can't be helped. She is as she is. Anyway, enough about my wayward child, let get on with the tour. I thought we would drive around the main house first, and then over to the other buildings and on down to where they are branding and vaccinating today how's that sound?"

Sarah nodded getting into the tour "That sounds great! This house is so large. Is it two or three stories high Alice?"

Actually it's only two stories what you are seeing and thinking is a third story is the attic. It is finished out over the west wing to be a bunkhouse of sorts. Except only the women hands are up there now, the guys opted to move back into the old bunk house, skunk or no skunk, when one of them found a box of tampons in the bathroom." Alice was chuckling "Or at least that's the story I got from one of the women. The male hands deny it though. They claim that they got tired of having to pick up after themselves."

Sarah was laughing too. She watched the landscape spread out before her as they drove around the west wing of the house along a nice gravel trail. Then they turned left into the formal gardens. The gardens stretched from the west wing to the east wing filling the space in between and bulging out into a semi-circle behind the house. From this angle Sarah realized that her first impression of the house as a square shape was wrong. It was actually more of a 'U'. Beyond the formal gardens was an area of wild flowers rolling down and away into some trees about a mile away or so. "Alice where does your property end?" she asked out of curiosity.

"Oh it's pretty large" she replied vaguely waving her hand toward the trees, "somewhere over that way a few days ride on a horse." Alice glanced at Sarah and said in a defensive tone, "well that's the farthest corner that way. The highway bounds the north side. And you saw the black fence we were driving along on the highway, well that's my fence. When it started that's where the west side of my property starts and it goes on east for a short distance. The house is tucked into the north east corner of my property."

Sarah thought back to when she had first noticed the black fence and realized that Alice's property had to be miles on a side. "Wow, that's really big." she said out loud "How do you get around? On horses?"

"Nah, we have a few jeeps and a helicopter to get around, horses take too long and they smell bad. Sometimes we do have to use them but not very often. If you like riding we do have a stable of horses. They are Jo's pride and joy you'll have to talk to her about which one's are OK to ride. Some of them are real frisky and even she has trouble controlling them."

Sarah's pulse quickened at the mention of Jo and she took a breath deciding that maybe she would try talking to this mysterious woman if only to dispel the vision in her head with reality. "Horses are a safe topic of discussion, really a perfect reason to talk to her since I can ride a little bit, though it has been a while," she thought to herself as they continued on their tour of the garden. Aloud she asked, "Where did this tree come from Alice?" admiring the big tree that was the central focus of the garden.

"Ah, the tree. Well now, that tree has a story and it goes like this. It was planted by my father, when he picked this very site for his homestead a good many years ago. Granted this house is not the house that he built, actually this is the third house that has been built in this very same spot. The first house he built was hardly more then a shack and as soon as he could he built one that was a bit larger and less leaky in bad weather. That second house was the house I grew up in. When he died and left me and my husband this ranch, I was his only child so everything came to me, mother died long before he did, the first thing my husband did was have that huge thing built," she said waving at the house with her left arm, "said that if we were going to live up here in the middle of nowhere that by god he was going to live in a house fit for a king. He never was too smart with money." Alice said shaking her head sadly "Oh, but I'm way off subject. The tree was planted by my father when it was still a seedling and long before he was married much less me being around. I'm not even sure how old it is exactly." They abandoned the cart for a time and wondered the garden. After a good thirty minutes of deep discussion on the different plants Alice had planted this year and lots of pointing to small metal name tags pushed into the ground near most of the plants, what birds were attracted by which plants and which ones might be viable in Houston, they climbed back into the buggy. Leaving the garden they headed east onto the path leading back to the front around the east wing. She noticed as they passed that all of the doors to the dinning hall were open letting the cool breeze run through the place.

Alice noticed her gaze and smiled "I have Maria air it out every day she can because of all of those stinky work-hands...me included in years past...eating in there every morning and night...leaves a smell behind after a while, kinda like a gym locker room only dustier with an undercurrent of beans." Sarah laughed at the description having not noticed it last night.

She watched quietly as they neared the stables hoping to see Jo while she was with Alice. Hoping Alice would introduce them. But Sam was the only person around and he was busy as they drove through the large side doors into the main part of the stable and out the back side of the building. Around the back of the stables they went, Alice giving the whole story as they rode along. Back through the stables and on to the east. "There'" Alice pointed out the bunk house that the guys had moved back out to. It seemed quite nice Sarah thought, and further out to the barn that sat on a hill a good half mile from the main house. Beyond the barn there were a bunch of pens and in those pens was where the action was happening. Sarah watched in fascination as they moved the young cows one by one through a narrow chute and trapped them, squeezing them in so they couldn't move, then vaccinated and branded them. Then they opened the chute and let that cow out into open pasture and moved the next cow into the tight space. It went very quickly. Sarah could have watched all day but Alice turned the golf cart and was on her way back to the main house. "Well, it's almost 5:00 and we can't be late for dinner." Alice said as they headed back.

"What about the, uh, hands?" Sarah asked unsure of the terminology.

"Oh they'll drive their trucks over to the house, it'll only take them a minute and they won't clean up before dinner except to wash their faces and hands. So they'll keep working for another thirty minutes or so." Alice continued her story of the place until they reached the stable again. There she deftly turned the golf cart right into the stables and then immediately left into one of the horse stalls next to an identical cart. After getting out she pulled a heavy cord out of the corner and plugged it into the cart explaining that they were always charged and ready to go that way.

Sarah and Alice walked together back to the house and up the stairs where they parted company at Sarah's door. Sarah walked into her room after watching Alice head down the hall to her room. She loved her princess room and as she walked through it she patted the happy colors of the pillows that were everywhere. She looked out the French doors toward the stables hoping to catch sight of Jo but she didn't see anyone. So she turned the handle and walked out onto the deck. Next to the door was a small patio set of four chairs and a table and over closer to the rail there was a small table and lounge chair sitting in the sun dapples. Further down there were more sets of furniture in front of two more doors before the deck curved away around the east wing of the house. Sarah walked back into her room and decided on a quick rinse off. "Maybe this evening I'll wear my favorite sweater to dinner," she thought to herself and a pair of my nicer jeans. "Maybe I'll pull my hair up too." she thought with visions of Jo filling her eyes, she quickly shook her head and lied to herself "I'm only doing it because I have a little time to burn." After her shower she put on a pair of black jeans and her favorite sweater, a dark emerald green pull over made of the softest cashmere that she found at her favorite resale shop for a song, and pulled her boots back on. Then she spent a few minutes fiddling her hair into a pile on top of her head. "There, I look much more presentable tonight." she thought, inspecting herself approvingly.

She headed down to the dinning room to find a few people beginning to drift in early and asked Maria if she needed any help. Maria put her to work helping Rosa set the long table without a second thought. Sarah and Rosa made short order of that project and moved on to filling the glasses with iced tea and getting serving dishes of hot food out onto the table. Everyone sat down and dinner began. Once again Sam was at Sarah's side talking with her and pulling her gently into friendly conversation. If he noticed Sarah's cleaner more nicely dressed appearance and her frequent furtive glances down the table at Jo he didn't mention it.

Jo sat by Alice and they talked jovially everyone seemed glad to see her including her mother. She had her hat off and Jo's short wavy black hair was finger combed back, but one curly lock kept falling into her face only to be brushed away again and again absently by Jo's strong fingers. Sarah memorized Jo's sparkling dark eyes, high cheekbones and the strong planes of her face, the way her dark hair framed her tan face, her quick smile and white teeth so she could draw her later in her sketch pad. Once, Jo turned her head quickly in Sarah's direction and caught her, those intense eyes pinning Sarah in her seat. Finally with a hard amusement, sparkling in her eyes Jo looked away again dismissing Sarah and resuming her animated discussion with the female work hand next to her. Everyone laughed. Sarah flushed and wished she had some idea what was going on behind those incredible, cool dark eyes. Sarah tried to pick up the thread of her conversation with Sam only to find him looking at her and then at Jo in a speculative way, deepening Sarah's flush to a deep blush.

Towards the end of dinner Jo stood up and announced "See you later. I'm headed into town to visit Sally. Anyone need anything?" A chorus of answers came back amidst lots of winks and jabs. Alice seemed withdrawn from the general joking and offered Jo her cheek for a peck in an automatic and distant way. Abruptly Jo turned before heading out the doorway and looking into Sarah with those fiery eyes said to Alice and the room "Maybe I should take Sarah along with me. What do you think mom? She might have a good time." Alice's eyes flashed mild annoyance at Jo. Jo continued looking into Sarah's eyes "Do you want to come along?" there was the briefest of pauses where their souls touched and then Jo's eyes widened slightly and she continued almost breathing her name "Sarah?" Everyone else in the room looked at Sarah and burst out laughing.

One of the women yelled out at Jo "Girl you are barking up the wrong tree. Hey, say Hi to Sally for me."

Sarah had no idea what all of the laughter was about but she laughed too not knowing what else to do.

"another time then maybe" Jo said bowing slightly she turned and strode out of the room and down the hall and was gone around the corner, leaving some of the work hands glancing at Sarah and chuckling.

Much later, after the house was dark and still, Sarah still was thrashing around unable to sleep. Instead visions of Jo and her, impossible dreams, filled her mind. Finally with much annoyance Sarah got up, got dressed and headed down to the kitchen for something to calm her down "Maybe a nice hot cup of tea will help." she thought to herself. "Who is Sally? Why was everyone laughing when Jo suggested taking me along? I don't think that was so crazy, after all Jo looks to be around my age. Maybe we would have had a good time together." Sarah shook her head in frustration knowing that everyone around her knew something about Jo that she did not. Silently she padded down the long curve of the stairs. She was about to pass Alice's study when the phone rang out loudly startling her. Pausing she waited for someone to pick up or an answering machine to catch it, but it just kept ringing. Finally after about eight rings Sarah advanced into the study and picked up the phone. "Hello?" she asked into the receiver.

From the other end came a huge racket and a man's voice yelling over the top of it all "Hey, Hello someone has got to come and get Jo. She's had way too much to drink and she's starting to throw things again. If she stays here much longer she'll be spending the night in jail for drunk and disorderly which she is...both, OK?"

Sarah instantly decided that she would go and get Jo reasoning with herself it was just because she did not want to wake up Alice and get her all upset, but knowing it was to find out where Jo had gone and why that was so funny to everyone. She got directions from the guy and headed out into the night looking for a vehicle and keys. She saw a light from the stable and realized it was coming from the office. As she got closer she could see Sam bent over the desk working on something. "Hi Sam, I don't mean to bother you so late but I can't sleep and thought that I might go for a drive." she lied. "I was wondering if I could borrow a car." He glanced up at her with surprise and indicated a rack of keys "How about one of the Jeeps? They are good for clearing the cobwebs. You can drive a stick shift right?" he asked pausing long enough to see her nod her head yes. "Grab the keys on the far end that's the Jeep closest to the front on the side of the stable over there." he pointed around the edge of the stable and Sarah thanked him and headed over to the line of Jeeps.

It started up without any trouble and off she went hoping that her midnight drive didn't seem too odd. About an hour later she arrived in front of a small bar, nearly frozen even with the heater running full blast on her feet. "He could have given me one with a roof at least" she thought to herself looking at her wild hair in the mirror. Out of the Jeep and into the bar she went, not knowing what to expect. There were a few people scattered about and a jukebox playing in the corner. A few women were gathered around the one pool table, laughing and having a good time. Two older ladies were out on the dance floor dancing together, holding each other in a relaxed closeness. "This is a lesbian bar," Sarah thought to herself suddenly understanding all of the undertones at dinner and blushing a little, her heart pounding at the implications suddenly swirling in her head. She took a deep breath and continued looking around. Jo wasn't hard to spot sitting hunched over at the bar with a sandy haired woman who seemed to be glancing around waiting for someone to show up and talking to Jo. The sandy haired woman spotted Sarah and inspected her with mild interest as she approached the two of them. Sarah walked up to Jo and nervously stood behind the two of them, "Um...Hi" she said "Someone called and said Jo might want a ride home." The bartender looked over Sarah with open curiosity and a touch of surprise and the sandy haired woman next to Jo smiled an open friendly smile and said "Hey, I'm Sally. Sally said. Sticking her hand out she added "If I didn't have company, I would have just brought Jo home with me for the night. Lord knows she has slept on my couch often enough."

Sarah took Sally's hand and smiled feeling more comfortable, it had been a long time since she had been in a women's bar, not since college, but she has quite a few friends in Houston that were lesbians so it was no big deal to her, "I'm Sarah. I'm a friend of Jo's mother and happened to be up to catch the call." By this time Jo had managed to turn around and silently regarded Sarah with open surprise.

"Well, you're not who I thought they'd send." Jo slurred trying to focus on Sarah "No you are definitely not who I thought would be coming to get me." Jo reached out and caught Sarah around the waist and pulled her firmly toward her, "Well, why don't you join us for a drink or two since you are here...Sarah." Her eyes steadied on Sarah's soft lips. "She is beautiful." Jo thought, "How can she be so unbelievably beautiful and when I looked at her at the dinner table tonight there was that connection. I know it was there. It was there from across the drive." Jo thought. "God she is beautiful, and she smells so good. Please let there be something wrong with her. Please let there be something wrong with this gold digger friend of mom's. Something about those eyes of hers, though, she is just wide open...as if she has nothing to hide." Jo shook her head confused by her own thoughts and pulled Sarah more firmly against her own hard body.

Sarah laughed nervously and tried casually and unsuccessfully to extricate herself from Jo's firm hold, "Oh, no someone has to drive you home and tonight it's going to be me," she said trying not to look into Jo's hypnotic eyes "so let's go." She tried to sound more certain then she felt. Jo's strong hands on the small of her back and the place where Jo's thighs were rubbing on either side of her hips now that Jo had pulled her even closer was doing terribly strange things to her pulse. She caught her breath trying again to focus on Sally and away from those powerful hands holding her. She took a breath, "Can she even walk?" she asked trying to sound as casual as she could under the circumstances and wondering how she would ever get Jo into the house once back at the ranch. Sarah knew, strong as she was, that her slim frame was no match for Jo's powerful build.

"I can walk fine." Jo said abruptly releasing Sarah, standing up and swaying. Once standing, Jo swayed, lost her balance and grabbed for Sarah, catching her, she pulled Sarah against her fully while trying to avoid the floor. Sally jumped up and grabbed Jo's side. Together Sarah and Sally stabilized Jo and got her headed out to the Jeep.

Sarah felt as if her skin were on fire where they had collided. She was no longer steady on her own feet. Sally wound up helping Jo walk out to the Jeep Sarah pointed out. Once Jo released her Sarah just stood by on wobbly knees watching as Sally pushed Jo into the passenger seat of the vehicle and got her strapped in. Then Sarah got into the driver side and started the jeep engine up, giving the heater a chance to get going before leaving.

Sally came around to Sarah's side of the Jeep and said, "You're doing fine." and patted her on the shoulder. "Don't pay Jo any mind. She's just having a bad time right now. She'll pull through it and be a lot nicer, you'll see."

Sarah smiled at Sally liking her friendly straightforwardness and with a wave bye pulled out of the parking lot and headed back to the ranch.

Jo watched Sarah for a long time in silence before she said anything "So you into rescuing damsel's in distress, Sarah?" Jo chuckled trying to take her boots off in the confines of the Jeep. Sarah did not immediately reply. Instead she was trying to slow her racing heart and breath. Jo at fifty yards was one thing but Jo only two layers of shirt fabric away was quite another and she knew at that moment even if she tried to refuse to admit it that this woman affected her like no one else ever had.

Trying desperately to keep Jo from stripping right there, in the Jeep and drive, occupied her for a good distance. So she did not answer Jo's question immediately. She could feel Jo's deep dark eyes on her.

Interpreting her silence as disgust Jo became uncommunicative and still "She must think I'm a real jerk. What does she know about me anyway? She's just a gold digger anyway, what do I care what she thinks?" Jo thought to herself sullenly.

After she settled down Sarah glanced at Jo and answered her question from earlier surprising Jo out of her silence "No, I'm not in the saving women business. I just happened to be up when the phone rang. You're in some shape." she said reprovingly "What would your mother think?"

"Aw hell, Sarah, she knows how I am." Jo said slapping the seat and chuckling in amusement. Sarah wanted to yell "stop saying my name or you are going to make me drive right off of this road from distraction!" But instead she scowled and didn't say anything. Jo slipped into silence thinking, "She hates me. The gold digger hates me. I'm such a jerk."

Sarah grateful for the quiet concentrated on driving the jeep. After a very cold quiet drive, they were home and Jo was out of the car and headed off away from the house. Sarah chased after her trying to head her back towards the house to no avail. Sarah was just no match for Jo's size and strength even though she was nearly 5'6" Jo towered over her. So she followed along trying to talk her into returning to the house, "This is what it must be like to attempt cat herding." Sarah thought in frustration, her breath coming in gasps of frosty air as Jo began stripping. First the hat, then the shirt and sports bra, her boots and socks were in Sarah's hands from the Jeep and as Jo continued to cast off clothes Sarah picked them up and kept walking after Jo saying things like "Come on Jo, it's way to cold to do what ever you have in mind," Jo laughing and chiding her all of the way disregarded her. Jo disappeared around a small building and as Sarah came around it "probably the pump shed" she thought to herself. She abruptly stopped dead in her tracks at the sight of Jo's nude sculpture perfect body in the full moon light at the end of a short dock. Jo was beautiful. Her hard, lean body abruptly arched in a shallow dive into a cow watering pool. She came up about half way across and she stood up running her hands through her hair, the moon light silvering off of her steaming body, she yelled for Sarah to come on in and join her. Sarah dropped Jo's clothes in a pile on top of her jeans, threw her hands up in exasperation and turned, leaving Jo swimming and singing loudly and yelling after her.

"Insufferable woman" Sarah thought as she headed back to the house heart pounding. She left the sounds of water splashing and a bawdy version of row row row your boat behind her in the darkness. She went up to her room and drew for a short time, then laid down thinking "Surely I should be able to sleep now out of shear exhaustion." When sleep finally did come to Sarah it was filled with dreams of Jo repeatedly coming up out of a pool of water and pulling Sarah into her arms.

Chapter 4

When Sarah awoke the next morning she spent a while sitting in bed thinking about a relationship long put out of her mind that she had in college with a woman. It was so intense and wonderful that, frightened of her feelings, she had finally broken it off refusing even to talk to Judy. Even though she had called repeatedly and sent Sarah flowers. Those feeling had been strong and had rocked the foundation of her understanding of herself. Sarah quietly sat and remembered. Realizing that she had never felt anything as strong as that with any of the men she had dated "Is that what it is to be a lesbian?" Sarah thought to herself letting the word and all of its connotations roll over her. "That was a lesbian bar Jo was in last night" she thought. "I know it was." She said it out loud to herself thinking of the connotations of that statement. "Jo is a lesbian," she thought knowing it for fact. "Am I feeling these things for Jo because…" she left the sentence unfinished, eyes wide at the thoughts running through her head this morning.

These were new thoughts, redefining thoughts, life changing thoughts. Even when she had been in that relationship with Judy all of those years ago, she had not thought about the implications of the depth of emotion she felt. Instead she had willed it away and when it would not go away she had run from it. Now though, she was much older and could look squarely at the reverberating implications and not be frightened by them. Instead she felt a strange sense of exhilaration, a coming into herself, a new understanding of many small past experiences. She got dressed in her running clothes and letting her mind jump around where it would, wandered down stairs for some coffee. "I need a good long run this morning and then some quiet time to think about all of this except maybe I'll do some more sketching."

There in the dining room was Jo, hunkered down with a cup of coffee and what looked like a bad hang over.

Sarah laughed silently, her heart skipping "Good for her, probably nursing one hell of a hang over, she earned it." Aloud she said, "Well, good morning. I hope you enjoyed your swim," she added as she went passed her into the kitchen for some coffee. Sarah came back out and sat down where Jo pointed.

"Yea, I was a little drunk last night." Jo conceded. She glanced sideways at Sarah and down at her coffee.

Sarah, realizing that was as much thanks as she could expect chuckled and said "I think you owe me now, big time."

Jo was thrown off guard by Sarah's good humor and looked at her deeply suspicious through narrow dark slits "Why, what do you have in mind?"

Since Jo didn't say no, Sarah abruptly decided to throw caution out the window and forged ahead "I hear you are the one to talk to about horses around here."

Jo nodded visibly relaxing a bit "That would be true."

"Well I was thinking that maybe you could give me a horseback tour of some of the ranch that you can't get to in a golf cart this afternoon." Sarah said holding her breath while Jo thought it over.

"I guess that would be a fair trade." Jo replied, surprised by the request, thinking that the last thing Sarah would want was time alone with her after her behavior last night. Unable to forget the feel of Sarah's body against hers but still suspicious of Sarah's motives she replied, "Okay, Sarah, I'll show you around. I didn't know you knew how to ride."

"I'm okay, not great, but it has been a while since I've been on a horse. What time do you want to meet up?" She asked trying to sound as casual as she could with her heart beating madly against her ribs.

"Oh, how about 10:30 or so" Jo said warming to the idea "I'll rustle up something to eat for lunch." Thinking to herself "Maybe I'll find out what she is really up to now, probably trying to scam mom out of some money. God, if only she wasn't so nice and so pretty."

"Okay, That'll give me plenty of time for my morning run and to get changed. Where should I meet you?"

"Oh, I'll be down by the stables." Jo replied watching Sarah get up with a dancer's smooth grace.

"Okay," Sarah said putting her cup away. "See you then. At least with you here, I don't have to worry about getting run over on the road." Sarah quipped on her way out the door.

"Oh, ha ha" Jo replied, "Very funny. If you weren't in the middle of the road I wouldn't have had to swerve to miss you." She hollered down the hall after her. "What a nervy woman." thought Jo with annoyance, admiring Sarah in spite of herself. She knew that Sarah had not told Alice about that incident or last night and wondered why "if she were after mom's money, surely she would be using those things to try and drive a wedge between us."

As Sarah went around the corner of the hall towards the front door, she ran into Alice. "Ah, just the person I was looking for." Alice said as she paused in the hall by Sarah, "I have to go into town for the day to visit my lawyer, take care of some banking details and over see the unloading of a bull we just bought. I always do that, probably no real reason to, but it is so exciting to me!" she looked concerned "If you are running out of things to do here, you could come into town with me and I could drop you where there are some good stores and pick you up later."

Sarah smiled "Oh, that's okay. Jo is going to give me a horse back tour of the ranch today Alice. After my morning run that is, I've gotta get going. You don't have to try to keep me entertained. The scenery alone can do that. Besides you know I'm not much of a shopper. Thanks for inviting me though."

Alice scowled and then smiled "Well what ever dear, don't let Jo be too hard on you. She can be a real tyrant. I hope you have a nice time."

"Thanks Alice, I'm sorry we haven't had much time to spend with each other but it seems like this ranch takes a lot of hands on managing."

"Oh it really does, to keep it moving along relatively crisis free." Alice said as she walked into her office. "Well I'll see you this evening then. Maybe after dinner we can have a game of Scrabble. I'm glad you're finding things to do," she said looking relieved and worried all at the same time.

"This place is great. The Scrabble game sounds great. I'll see you this evening, then." Sarah said as she walked out the front door.

Her run was uneventful except for the jarring motion of her mind. And in the center of that vortex was Jo who she was about to go out into the country with. She knew that Jo could take care of herself and knew this land very well, and she wasn't worried about that. Instead she was confused and excited about her own feelings for Jo. They were so strong. And it seemed obvious to her that Jo did not have any strong feelings for her except maybe as entertainment. "If I were Jo, and a woman around my age became friends with my mother over the Internet, what would I think? If she tried to be friends with me what would I do?" Sarah wondered having no clear answers to her questions. After her run she went up stairs took a quick shower and changed into her old jeans, boots, and a flannel shirt with a T-shirt underneath. Hurriedly, she brushed her hair out and then pulled it up and back into a ponytail. Down the stairs and out to the stables she went, "I know I'm a little early but, oh well. What the hell." she thought to herself.

Once she got to the stables, she wandered around looking for Jo until they, quite literally, almost ran into each other. Jo was carrying a small cooler in one hand containing their lunch and striding along when Sarah stepped around a corner and they very nearly collided. Sarah put her hands out expecting to get run over, but Jo stopped abruptly leaving Sarah's hands resting lightly on her hard stomach just above Jo's jeans.

"I'm here with the food" Jo said, her voice coming out a bit lower and huskier then she intended. She hefted a little cooler in absentminded demonstration, very aware of Sarah's warm hands and light touch through the thin fabric of her T-shirt. She slowly looked down at Sarah's hands. "What kind of game is she playing with me anyway?" she thought to herself.

Sarah in embarrassment said, "Oh, I'm sorry. I should have been paying closer attention to where I was going." Jo was looking down at something and following her gaze down Sarah discovered to her shock that she still had her hands resting against Jo's stomach. Sarah quickly pulled them away, and spinning on her heal to hide her embarrassment, nearly fell over an old saddle.

Jo reached out with her free hand instantly and without thinking, caught Sarah around her waist pulling Sarah back towards her to keep her from falling. Holding Sarah steady, Jo noticed how shaky she was and wondered "Are you that nervous around me after last night Sarah?" but couldn't bring herself to release Sarah's firm softness and so Jo lightly held onto Sarah breathing in her scent and feeling Sarah's body lean back against her for support. Jo leaned down and, heart pounding, nuzzled Sarah's soft hair, making Sarah breath in sharply. Just for a moment Sarah yielded to Jo and lean against her fully, then she seemed to regain her intention and pulled away a little.

Jo released her reluctantly but a chuckle came up out of her and then warm laughter that only made Sarah all the more embarrassed and confused. Jo thought to herself with sharp amusement "Whatever she has got in mind when it comes to mom's money, she may successfully drive me insane in the process too." she continued to chuckle to herself but said out loud to Sarah's graceful retreating back. "Slow down woman, you are going to hurt yourself. The horses will wait. They have all day." and under her breath she added "and so do I."

"Maybe this was a mistake," Sarah thought to herself "How am I going to ride a horse if I can't even walk with her near me? And what was I doing back there? It just felt so right to be in her arms. You've got to pull yourself together or she's going to think you are a crazy woman, Sarah." she thought taking several breaths. Sarah turned to find Jo gone again. "Jo? Jo where are you?" Sarah called into the stable.

"I'm over here." Jo called out, "by the corral."

Sarah saw Jo, one boot hooked over the lower rail, lunch cooler on the ground and both arms resting lightly on the top rail "those broad shoulders of hers should be illegal." Sarah thought ruefully as she approached, careful not to trip over anything else she walked up and stood beside Jo looking out at the horses. Jo glanced at her the turned and faced her "Well, do you see anything that strikes your fancy...Sarah?"

Sarah looked at Jo's laughing dark eyes and out to the horses not sure if Jo meant anything by the wording of her last question or not.

But decided to take it at face value and immediately pointed out a beautiful shiny chestnut colored mare with a black mane and tail and a white blaze on her forehead. "Oh that one if I could ride her, I would love it."

Jo inspected Sarah momentarily thinking, "Maybe too much horse for this woman." she cautiously asked Sarah "How much riding have you done?"

Sarah looked at the horse and back to Jo with annoyance "You don't think I can ride her?" she accused.

Jo backed down "Okay, okay I didn't mean anything by the question. It's just that the horse you picked is a bit spirited and needs a good rider is all. But I'll saddle her up if you're set on her."

Sarah nodded a 'yes' at Jo stubbornly refusing to believe that such a beautiful animal could be that hard to ride.

Jo moved into the corral and retrieved the mare and another horse and got them saddled up while Sarah watched. Her motions were fluid and the horses seemed to have no fear of her. While she worked, Jo talked quietly to them and they seemed to softly whicker back at her in conversation.

"Okay, here you go." Jo said. "Sarah meet Lady Fire, Lady Fire meet Sarah. This here horse is my favorite. His name is Chester Cheetos because of his color."

Sarah laughed in delight and climbed into her saddle in one smooth motion. Jo watched her approvingly and climbed into her own. Jo turned her horse and they began moving off to the southwest, allowing the horses to set their own pace while Jo told Sarah about the ranch and her father. After a pleasant lunch by a stream that ran through the property from northwest to southeast, Jo casually pulled Sarah into talk about Alice. And Sarah told her all about meeting Alice in a world news chat room and how much they had in common and how their friendship had grown and coming out here and what a shock it had been that Alice was so wealthy.

Jo snorted saying "Surely you knew she was well off before you came up here."

Sarah stiffened at Jo's unstated suggestion that Alice's money had something to do with their friendship and responded "I had no idea. Your mother hadn't mentioned it and I had never asked. Besides money just isn't an issue I think about when it comes to friendship."

"Oh yea, right. Mother didn't mention she was wealthy." Jo said laughing at Sarah in partial disbelief, but part of her thought "It sounds like something my mother would do, not mention her money, and if that is true than Sarah came up here just to visit mom and not her money. That would be a nice change."

Absolutely furious that Jo would believe that her friendship with Alice was based on Alice's money, Sarah stood up from where they were sitting by the stream, spun around and stormed off to the horses, climbed up on to Lady Fire. "If that is what you think of me then I see no reason to continue this afternoon excursion, I'll see you back at the house, but only if I have to Jo!" she said and pulled on the reins to turn her horse. Lady Fire sensing the anger shooting through Sarah's veins was jumpy though, and when Sarah pulled on the reins, instead of turning smoothly she sidled herself off the edge of the shallow bank of the stream. Jo seeing what was about to happen and unable to get to the horse in time was already up when the horse reared violently and threw Sarah into the rocky stream bed before galloping away.

"Damn, damn, damn." Jo said under her breath, hurrying over to where Sarah lay on the rocks in the shallow water. Her pace increased as she realized that Sarah was not getting up. She was not moving. "Not again." She ran the last few steps to Sarah's side in the water and dropped down on her knees beside Sarah, oblivious to the icy cold soaking up her jeans "Please be okay, Please be okay. I'm sorry, Sarah. I believe you."

Sarah began turning her head from side to side and mumbling something as Jo leaned over her. Carefully, Jo began going over Sarah's whole body inspecting for breaks and finally Sarah's eyes opened and focused on Jo. "Hey you all right?" Jo asked softly, deep concern laced with fear cut in her eyes.

Sarah just stared at her without recognition for a while and then as her mind cleared a little, her eyes took on a bruised expression as she remembered Jo's accusation. "I'm fine. I'm just a little shaken up is all." She said in an almost inaudible voice. "What happened?" she asked as she tried to sit up and discovered she was in the stream, soaked to the bone and very cold.

"Oh Lady Fire threw you into the stream and rode away home." Jo said trying to sound casual as she continued her inspection of Sarah. "Does this hurt?" she asked rotating Sarah's arm.

"Not too much, no." Sarah replied through chattering teeth. Letting Jo move her arms and then her legs, her entire body feeling like one big aching bruise. Sarah was not sure if the pain was because of what Jo had assumed or the fall in her grogginess.

"Okay let's get you out of the stream. What do you say, Sarah." Jo said getting her arms around Sarah and pulling her up onto her feet. As soon as Jo had Sarah up, Sarah groaned and sagged heavily against Jo, "Just take it slow Sarah, you had quite a fall." Jo coaxed. Tentatively Sarah took two steps and with an almost inaudible apology in Jo's ear passed out. Jo caught her easily and lifted her up into her arms.

Chester stood stoically by saying nothing, but giving Jo that "Look what you have done now." look, while Jo tried to coax Sarah back into consciousness "Come on Sarah, come on sweet Sarah, open your eyes for me, come on back to me, Sarah." Sarah's dark eyelashes moved against her cheeks and finally, she did open her eyes again. Jo leaned her against Chester and was in the saddle in one motion. Immediately she leaned over and pulled Sarah up onto her lap, both of them thoroughly soaked now. After some fiddling Jo got Sarah tucked in across her lap with Sarah's head resting against her shoulder, conscious or not Jo had a hold of her. Jo clicked her tongue at Chester and he started off at an easy pace. Jo wouldn't take him any faster with two people on his back and with Sarah unconscious again. "Why did you let her ride that horse Jo?" Jo asked herself angrily "You must have hoped she would hurt herself and being the sweet woman that she obviously is she obliged you." Feeling Sarah's softness rubbing against her with every step of the horse Jo cursed herself and Sarah under her breath "Why in hell did you have to become friends with my mother, why couldn't you be friends with someone else's mother instead." Sarah's long hair, having fallen out of its ponytail, hung damply, framing her face, making her look even paler and more vulnerable. Jo quietly accused herself of terrible things, while she tried to focus on riding the horse and not on Sarah's intoxicating scent and the heat their bodies made through their wet clothes.

Sarah slowly regained consciousness, to find herself sitting across Jo's lap, leaning against her. With vague thoughts of being helpful she slid her loose arm around Jo's neck, pulled herself up against Jo and held on, resting her head against one of Jo's strong shoulders.

Jo immediately noticed Sarah's movement and stiffened as Sarah turned more fully against her bringing her breasts against Jo's. "Oh this, this is much more distracting." thought Jo to herself. "Please turn back around the way I had you," she silently begged, but the only response she got from Sarah was a soft nuzzling, her lips grazing Jo's neck. Jo's pulse raced and Sarah's warm regular breath against her throat melted her completely. Careful not to disturb Sarah, Jo switched the reins to her other hand and slid her phone out. She quietly dialed a number and spoke into the phone. "Yea Doc. It's Jo, Alice's guest fell off of a horse and I'm bringing her back to the main house now. Could you come up and take a look at her, nothing seems broken but she's out like a light. I should be back there in about thirty minutes. I'm just taking it slow I don't want to jar her too much." Jo listened for a few minutes and said, "Okay, then we'll expect you. Thanks." then pressed the end button on her cell phone and put it away. Sarah shifted a little and Jo slid a protective arm around her waist. Holding Sarah against her, Jo thought. "Ah, Sarah how dare you be so beautiful and so..." she left the sentence unfinished knowing that this line of thought was probably hopeless.

Sarah awoke much later to find herself in her bed. She looked around and noticed Jo leaning against the frame of her French glass doors looking out into the darkness of night beyond. Sarah watched Jo standing there, still in the clothes from their ride, looking ragged and strong and beautiful and remembered pieces of the afternoon and her fall and the reason for her fall. She felt emotionally bruised all over again. "Why, are you here?" she asked quietly breaking the silence of the room.

Jo spun around, deep in her own accusing thoughts she hadn't noticed Sarah stir. She moved across the room silent and lithe as a prowling mountain cat to stand next to Sarah's bed.

"I thought you hated me." Sarah accused painfully "You said I was only after your mother's money." She said more firmly as memories of the fight rolled over her. "You hate me. I just know you do and yet when I fell..."

Jo had decided while Sarah was sleeping that she wouldn't bring up the way Sarah made her feel, but now that Sarah was awake and looking at her with those soft emerald green eyes full of angry hurt Jo was helpless. "I caused all of this pain. I can be so stupid sometimes," she thought. Silently she leaned over Sarah and kissed her, softly on the mouth silencing Sarah in mid sentence. Sarah closed her eyes and kissed Jo back, knowing with absolute certainty, that this was what she had wanted more than anything else in the world since laying eyes on Jo. Sarah slid an arm around Jo's neck and pulled her down against her. Their lips melted together in an unquenchable fiery softness. Then Jo pulled away, stood up again to her full height and looked at Sarah with a deep sadness in her eyes that ended all discussion and left without explaining. Sarah drifted in and out of sleep for the rest of the night and awoke in the morning to breakfast in bed and every inch of her body stiff and sore. For the first time in years, Sarah conceded, she would not be running today before breakfast or after.

Alice checked in on her while she was still finishing the meal that Rosa had brought. Her eyes full of concern "Oh Sarah, I am so sorry. Are you Okay? Jo was so upset, feels like it is all her fault for some silly reason." Alice looked at her hoping for a denial, but obviously fearing that it was indeed somehow Jo's fault.

Sarah smiled at her friend, and remembered the soft kiss and Jo's hauntingly sad eyes. She wondered if it was a dream or not. "No Alice, I don't know why she thinks that. It was my own fault, she warned me about Lady Fire and I still insisted on riding her. This was all, my fault and I'm sorry she feels that way."

Alice seemed relieved "She stayed up here all afternoon and nearly half the night with you." Alice watched Sarah closely, "I don't know where she is now, but I'm sure she would be glad to know you were up and looking alive again. Doc. Peterson said you got a bit of a concussion and you're pretty bruised up and that you need to take it easy for a few days, but that you'll live."

There was a soft rapping on the door and Jo walked in, looking guilty of murder. Her eyes full of 'I'm sorrys,' she asked Sarah how she felt.

Alice noticing the emotional currents in the room and not knowing or wanting to know what was going on between them excused herself.

Sarah patted the side of the bed and Jo obediently walked over and sat down next to her. Sarah amazed at Jo's catlike grace said,

"Alice is right about you having the grace of a mountain lion." Jo looked at Sarah with surprise and Sarah realizing suddenly that she had said it aloud, blushed. Jo looked at Sarah with her dark eyes carefully shuttered revealing nothing except a quiet touch of amusement.

"So, how are you today?" Jo asked watching Sarah's every movement.

"I'll live." Sarah responded carefully, not knowing what to think this morning in the sunlight about last night's kiss.

"Good." Jo smiled nervously and continued to say nothing about the kiss, wondering if Sarah remembered it at all, and waiting for her to mention it first.

Sarah looked at Jo. She wanted Jo to kiss her again like she did in the moon light, wanted to feel Jo's arms around her again like at the stable, wanted to feel her body against Jo's like at the bar, wanted things that she couldn't even find words for. She had no idea how to talk about this. She sighed in frustration.

Jo scowled, "What's wrong, you look upset. Did I do something to upset you, Sarah? It is my fault that you fell off of the horse in the first place. But you don't understand what it is like having Alice for a mother. I had to know what your intentions were." She searched Sarah's face for understanding and then charged forward "I mean she is always taking in strays...I mean..." Jo stopped and looked at Sarah silently, a pained expression on her face and ended with. "I am sorry you fell off of Lady Fire." There was a long pause while Jo, eyes squeezed shut and knuckles white from gripping the sheet, tried to figure out if anything she had just said made any sense at all.

Sarah sat up gingerly bringing her face close to Jo's bowed head "But are you sorry you kissed me Jo? That is all I want to know." She said it so softly that Jo wasn't sure she had heard right or was just hoping. Opening her eyes and lifting her head she found Sarah's lips inches from hers "I remember Jo." Sarah added looking straight into Jo's dark eyes, feeling her heart racing at her own boldness and feeling lightheaded from sitting up and from Jo's closeness. It just didn't matter any more she had to know how

Jo felt.

Jo leaned back a little trying to find some bit of reality to hold onto before she fell completely and madly in love with this woman, but Sarah abandoning all pretenses slid her arms around Jo's neck. Letting the sheets slide, she leaned up not giving Jo a chance to do anything but respond. Jo let out a quiet groan of pleasure as the sheets slid down around Sarah's waist and the softness of her breasts were briefly revealed before Sarah leaned herself fully against Jo. Again their lips met in a meltingly soft kiss, eliciting another deep groan from Jo. "Why does she have to do every little thing right?" Jo thought trying to break through to reality again, instead Jo found herself lying Sarah back down and gently kissing her on the tender soft spots of her neck that she instinctively knew about. Across Sarah's forehead and her eyelids Jo allowed her mouth to explore Sarah's neck and shoulders before returning again to Sarah's mouth, which she kissed with less gentleness and more passion this time. Jo kissed Sarah again and again until she could have howled to the moon with her desire.

And Sarah was responding in kind, kissing Jo anywhere handy and then on her mouth again and again thinking, "Yes! This is how it should be. I love this woman. I love her." Abruptly Jo pulled away and stood up, taking several steps away from Sarah and breathing shallowly she said, "You have to think about this. The implications of what you are doing. I am not here for your vacation entertainment."

Sarah looked dazed, but said "Jo what are you talking about? I have thought about this. I have thought of hardly anything else but this." and she added more softly, "hardly anything else but you."

Scowling at her own heart's joyous leap at hearing these words Jo replied soberly "You still have to think about the implications, Sarah. I will not let you hurt me by abruptly changing your mind or something." Jo glanced at her watch and said, "I have to go now. We'll talk about this some more when I get back." and with that she was out the door.

The words when I get back rang out in Sarah's mind. "When I get back from where?" she wondered but Jo was already gone. Carefully shifting to a more comfortable position she thought in shock, "What am I doing? I practically threw myself at her." she thought as she self-consciously pulled the sheets back up around herself. "I have never acted like that before. But I wanted to feel her lips against mine again I had to. Maybe I should leave this place, just get away from here and get away from Jo. If I do leave what will Alice think?" a flood of self-doubt washed over her. "What am I doing falling in love with Alice's daughter?"

Sarah spent the day moving from the bed to the lounge chair on the deck and back again to her bed, her body complaining vigorously every time she moved. She sketched in her sketchpad and thought about what Jo had said the implications of her love. As an artist, she knew several lesbians and she knew that in some ways their life was harder, but in others it seemed to her that it was much richer and fuller. There was no inequality automatically built into their relationships. The couples she knew had been together for a long time and there was a bond there that she knew she could never share with a man. They shared an intimacy that she had envied that she knew came with the complete understanding of each others needs that could be shared by two women. Alice came by and visited with Sarah for a while in the afternoon and they played that Scrabble game. Then, the two of them sitting companionably on the deck in the sunny dappled shade enveloped in comfortable silence Sarah requested "Alice, tell me about Jo."

Alice looked at Sarah cautiously trying to decide what she meant. "Well, Jo is my only child. She was born and raised here on this ranch. I was quite old by the time I had her and it was a bit of a surprise. We had given up on the idea of having children by then. I have always run the ranch, my husband, bless his heart, just wasn't much of a businessman. So I guess it's no surprise that Jo grew up assuming that a woman could do anything. She is very capable and I know that when I die she'll do a fine job running this place. She went to school in town and did well, although she did get teased a lot for being so tall." Alice paused and then continued encouraged by her friend's look of quiet understanding. "I always thought that the reason she never dated boys was because she was always taller then they were, but now I think it was more then that. Now, I think the boys where intimidated by her ability to do anything that they could, often better then they could. And I think she never met a boy that impressed her enough to catch her interest. She got her degree in Agricultural Management. Even though she did not want to go, she got good grades and finished top of her class." she glanced nervously at Sarah, trying to judge what her friend thought about all of this.

Sarah noticed Alice's glance and realizing that she was waiting for a reply said, "I think that Jo is a very capable woman. Maybe you are right. Maybe she never did meet the right man." Sarah paused trying to decide if she was going to say anything else, then took a deep breath and continued knowing she had to. "But, I think it's possible that Jo just never liked boys that way too. Maybe she is just different like that."

Alice shifted uncomfortably "Maybe so. Who's to say these days. Maybe it's my fault for having her so late in life. I've heard theories about hormones and all. Maybe it's my fault. Maybe I should have spent more time teaching her how to be more feminine. But how could I? She was always out in the corral with the horses or off riding with her dad and I was always busy running this place, the consummate micro manager."

Sarah looked surprised "You mean that you think if you had taught your daughter to doubt herself more, and be less capable and worry about her looks and her abilities that somehow she would have been a better woman?"

Alice sighed heavily. "No, I am glad that Jo is so sure of herself and so very capable, what I wish is that she liked dresses and occasionally had her nails done. Or had longer hair or a hobby like quilting or some of the other things most women do." Alice paused "Do you know, I have never talked to anyone about any of this, Sarah. It is such a relief to finally say it out loud. My daughter, bless her, is a..." Alice took a deep breath, "a lesbian." Alice's voice was so low that Sarah had to lean towards her to hear "She is. I know she is. I wish it had turned out different. Is that so terrible? I wish she had married a nice intelligent man and had grandbabies for me to love and hold and I blame myself for not doing something or doing too much of something else." Alice stopped talking. She looked old and small and tired. There was a frailty to her that worried Sarah, and she reached out and took Alice's hand.

Holding Alice's hand, she thought about how her own mother would react to the news that her oldest daughter was finally in love but with a woman. She knew it would probably be rough. No mother holds her baby girl and prays "please lord let her be a lesbian, let her be discriminated against and harassed, let the church preach against her, let her get fired from jobs because of who she is, let the legislature pass laws against her too while you're at it just to make her life challenging." With deep sadness and a new understanding of what lay ahead, Sarah said "Oh, Alice, I think that if you were to talk to Jo about this, you would find that it was not your fault at all. That it had nothing to do with anything that you did or didn't do, but something down deep within her. Jo is just Jo, and probably down inside knew all along that she was attracted to women and not men."

Alice wiped a tear track away off of her tan cheek "I know I am selfish for wanting grandbabies. I know that part of me has tried to live my life through my hopes for Jo. Please don't get me wrong I do want her to be happy. I do love her very much. Ah, well. She is as she is." They sat together silently, each in their own thoughts for a long time. Then finally Alice broke the silence with a question as realization swept over her face "Sarah, you are in love with my daughter, aren't you?"

Sarah was startled by the directness of Alice's question "Why do you ask?" Sarah asked to give herself more time to decide how to answer.

Alice was watching her closely now with sharp sudden awareness in her eyes "I don't miss much around here Sarah. Tell me are you? I must know." her grip on Sarah's hand was very tight indeed.

It was Sarah's turn to shift in her seat. Finally meeting Alice's penetrating eyes with her own openness, she answered "I have never felt like this before about anyone, ever." Sarah paused knowing what was in her heart she finally continued, "Yes Alice, I am in love with your daughter." Sarah said looking Alice straight in the eyes ready to face the firing squad.

Alice nodded and didn't say anything, just squeezed Sarah's hand. They sat in silence holding on to each other's hand until the dinner bell rang and Alice stirred "Can't be late for dinner. Are you up to coming down tonight or do you want Maria to bring something up to you?"

"Oh, I think I'll creep on down for dinner, can't miss dinner." Sarah said smiling. Then Sarah added cautiously "If you want me to Alice, I'll leave. I'll go back to Texas and not come back." Doubting that she actually was willing to leave, Sarah held her breath waiting for Alice's reply.

"Oh, don't be silly, Sarah. You are my friend and are welcome here as long as I breathe. What goes on between you and Jo is just that, between you and Jo."

Sarah squeezed Alice's hand in relief and together they went down to dinner.

Chapter 5

Sarah awoke the next morning from a vivid dream in which Jo came up out of a dark mysterious pool, moonlight shimmering off of her wet body as she walked up to Sarah and then they were kissing over and over again, their bare flesh pressed against each other in a large, soft bed covered in dark satin sheets under the moon. She rose stiffly and sat on the side of the bed her world spinning from the dream that still was slipping from her eyes. As if she had an awake sensor in Sarah's room, Maria appeared with breakfast and a friendly quip about running, to which Sarah had to laugh. "Maria, she called from the bath room, would you please show me how to use this tub. It looks so complicated, all of these dials and buttons and spouts but I don't want to go back to Houston without enjoying at least one bath in it."

Maria, laughing all of the way into the room said, "I have never had to explain a bathtub before. Let's see you fill it with water, and get into the water and wash, and don't forget to wash behind your ears, then you get out of the water and drain the tub." She chuckled at her funny and Sarah laughed too. Then she showed Sarah how to fill it and turn the jets and heater on and how to drain it afterwards.

"There you go. Now you are officially bathtub certified!" Maria said and off she went to do other things.

Sarah nibbled on her breakfast while the huge tub was filling. Once it was full she turned on the jets and slid into the steamy hot frothing water, letting the motion of the water massage her strained muscles. "I'm feeling a good bit better today." she thought to herself, pleased. "I wonder where Jo is and when she will be back. I'll have to ask someone, I guess." She realized with a start that her trip was nearly half over. She would be going back to Houston in ten days. Right there and then she decided that she would go into town after supper and find that bar again, and spend the evening trying to have a good time with or without Jo. "Maybe it's not Jo." she thought "Maybe it's just women in general" but she knew in her heart that Jo was the one.

After her long bath, Sarah dressed in warm comfortable clothes and headed down into the day. She wandered about sketching, and photographing the hands doing their chores and putting their names under the sketches much to their amusement. She tried to get a grasp of spring leaves Montana style instead of Houston style. Knowing the whole time that whatever happened between Jo and herself, this trip would profoundly change the way she saw the world she painted and that she would have to return again and again to this compelling and rich landscape. After many hours outside and feeling drained, she finally headed back to the house to rest and to have a little snack of some sort. She found Alice in her office, staring at the wall in deep thought, and paused at the doorway hoping Alice would notice her. She did not so Sarah went on by wondering what had Alice's full attention and headed into the kitchen for a little bit of food. She made some orange spice tea while she hunted through the refrigerator for something to eat. Finding some left over refried beans, a block of cheese and flour tortillas, Sarah settled into a snack.

Deciding that she would drop in on Alice afterwards to see what was on her mind.

She let her mind wander around Jo and her new knowledge of herself while she ate. "I am a lesbian, I think. No, I know I am. I know I am a lesbian. That explains so much, why I loved the way my kindergarten teacher smelled and I loved how her soft honey blond hair felt when she leaned over me. Why I dressed my dog up in curtains and made him the bride for me to marry at my pretend wedding when I was four. My whole life makes so much more sense suddenly." Sarah thought shaking her head in disbelief that it took this long for her to figure it out. "I even have friends that are lesbian!" she thought about Barbara and Jodi at the gallery where her next art exhibit was going to be.

She finished her light meal, rinsed her dishes off and put them next to the sink. Then she walked back up to the front foyer to see if Alice was still in her office. Sarah had decided that talking with Alice would be a good way to clarify her own feelings and get her thoughts in order. "I sure miss Jo, but I'm glad she's not here today, so I can think this through." Sarah thought to herself as she walked to the doorway of Alice's office.

Alice looked up when Sarah approached this time and said "Well, Hello Sarah. I am so glad to see you up, out and about today. I see you have your sketchpad and camera with you. What have you been up to?"

Sarah replied with a smile "Oh, I have been out taking reference photos of your work hands much to their amusement, doing some quick thumb sketches of ideas for paintings and generally having a good old time. How about you Alice? I know that the other day we had a pretty serious talk. How are you doing?"

Alice looked at her friend and sighed, "You know, I have just been sitting here thinking about what we talked about the other day, and realizing some very difficult things about myself. Like just how hard

I have been on Jo. For example take the time I tried to make her go out with the son of one of the ranchers from my church, certain that they would hit it off, even though she was dating a lady pretty steady at the time and I knew it, but I just kept hoping that if she met the right man or that maybe it was a phase or something she would outgrow. And a whole host of other things I have done to make her life hard. Well, hell if I were Jo I probably would have left long ago and started my own ranch or something. But she has stuck it out and put up with my meddling and scowls for all of these years." Alice burst into tears without warning and through the tears asked Sarah "Do you think I am a bad mother, Sarah?" Alice sniffed and wiped her face on her sleeve. "I mean I thought I only wanted what was best for Jo, but now I'm realizing that maybe what I wanted was only my idea of what was best for her, not what really and truly was best for her. I think I had my own comfort set before her happiness." Alice looked at Sarah through tears waiting on an answer.

Sarah was at a loss for words for a while then after thinking about it replied, "Alice, I think you have been a wonderful mother to Jo. If you had not, she would not have stayed around and she would not be the person that she is. I think that the two of you need to talk about this though, not us. These are things that you need to tell Jo, something the two of you need to talk about."

Alice blew her nose loudly and wiped her eyes again, "You are right of course, I have not been a bad mother. But I have not been very good about letting Jo know how much I love her, and how proud of her I am. I am so very proud of her you know. She has learned this business inside and out, knows how to brand and vaccinate a cow, can tell you what they are selling for at any given moment, what the best feed is anything really. I should give her more responsibility around here, just sort of let her take the reigns and make helpful suggestions from the passenger's seat for a while. I know she can do it. Then I could rest and do some of the things I have wanted to do.

Maybe even come down and visit you in Houston for a little while, although I hear the air is bad and the heat is awful." Alice said with a little laugh.

Sarah laughed too knowing that Alice was quoting one of her recent emailed notes. The discussion smoothed into other topics and before they knew it they had talked the afternoon away. The supper bell rang and the two of them went off together to wash up and eat.

At supper she asked Sam as casually as she could "When will Jo be home?"

Sam inspected her with equal casualness and replied "Oh, she went to Germany to buy some semen from a bull she found on the Internet, said she'd be back tomorrow evening late sometime. Since she drove herself, no one has to go and pick her up this time." He looked pointedly at her and Sarah realized he was referring to the night Sarah had retrieved Jo from the bar, "She left her truck at the airport."

Then Jo's destination sank in "Germany." Sarah was surprised "Germany, as in Europe? Germany?"

Sam laughed at Sarah's surprise "Sure, we buy from all over the world, depending on the characteristics that we are trying to bring into the heard. This particular bull is a really good one. We've bought from him before and had really good results."

After dinner Sarah spent a good bit of time getting ready to go out. She did not want to look too dressed up compared to everyone else, but at the same time wanted to look nice. She discovered with some frustration that balancing the two ideas was more difficult then she expected.

Finally Sarah borrowed a Jeep, with a roof, and went into town. She parked in front of the small bar and sat there for some time looking at the cars in the parking lot and trying to figure out if Sally might be there before going in. She didn't see a car she thought would be Sally's, but went in anyway. There were more people in the bar this time, but she spotted Sally leaning against the bar in almost the same spot and watching people. Sarah walked over towards Sally who noticed her and smiled a friendly smile and said, "I remember you. You saved Jo from jail the other night. What was your name again?"

"I'm Sarah" Sarah replied, "Do you mind if I join you?"

Sally continued to smile but a touch of polite caution came into her voice "Sure, help yourself to a stool. So are you having a nice stay? Visiting Alice, right? You here with Jo tonight?" Sally asked with obvious cautious curiosity about Sarah, "I thought she was in Germany."

"No, Jo is not here with me. She is in Germany. At least that is where Sam said she was this evening at supper." Sarah said, trying to sound casual. "I thought I would come down here and just unwind. It has been a crazy few days." Sarah replied.

"I can believe you there. So do you dance?" Sally asked.

Sarah paused and Sally caught it immediately, "It's just a dance girl. That isn't cheating or anything. I don't care if you already have a sweetie. I'm not looking for anything anymore, I just love to dance."

Sarah feeling reassured, and liking Sally's friendly round face, replied "Sure, okay, but go easy on me, I'm a bit stiff and sore." and off to the small dance floor they went. Several pairs of eyes followed them out, but there was no hostility in any of them, only open curiosity. Soon the dance floor had several couples on it. One old couple seemed to be in their own little happy world. Sally caught Sarah watching them "Oh, that's Frances and Jill. They have been together longer then this world has been around I figure. Frances is a retired deputy sheriff, and Jill used to teach at the local school, now they own a little spread about twenty minutes west of here. Sometimes they will invite everyone over for a big barbecue. They're good people. It's disgusting how much they like each other. I have heard rumors that they have fought, but I think it is just wishful thinking by jealous people."

Sarah laughed as she watched the old couple sway in time to the music. Thinking, "They sure do fit together like they were made for each other." out loud she said "So give me the scoop on everyone else in here Sally." Her curiosity aroused.

"Oh you get to go first." Sally replied a glimmer of mischief shining in her merry eyes.

"What could I possibly have to tell, that you would want to know?" Sarah asked surprised and a bit nervous. She tensed suddenly, wondering if Jo had talked to this woman about her behavior before leaving for Germany.

"Oh, I think you can start by telling me all about what happened the night you came and got Jo." Sally's eyes laughed but inside she was curious about Sarah's obvious nervousness.

Sarah heaving a sigh of relief, related the whole evening down to the bawdy row row row your boat song, swim in the cow tank, and the next morning with Jo drinking her coffee and her hang over. They both laughed out loud about it all. She didn't go on to tell her newly found friend about the horse ride or the kiss though.

Then Sally told funny stories about everyone in the room she knew including herself, explaining to Sarah she would hear them anyway if she were to ask any one else in the room. By the end of the evening Sally had introduced Sarah around to everyone there that she knew. Sarah had danced several dances and had drunk more than she cared to think about. Sally, noticing how tipsy Sarah was suggested in her motherly tone, that Sarah should stay at her place until morning, since it was a long drive out to the ranch and Sally's company had gone home again so the couch was once again available for drunken friends.

And Sarah throwing all caution to the wind decided to accept. Sally's place was a small house nearly within walking distance of the bar. It was tidy, clean and very spare. Sally watched Sarah look over her place and said, "I know it's not much, but I like it. A real come down from the Thompson spread for you I bet."

Sarah looked embarrassed, "That is not what I was thinking." she said.

"Oh, what were you thinking?" Sally asked watching her casually as Sarah flopped down on the futon couch and began to pull her boots off.

"I was thinking that your place looks a lot like mine back home in Houston." Sarah replied smiling and feeling a little homesick in spite of herself. "Hope my little kitty is doing okay." Sarah thought.

This caused Sally to reassess Sarah and she said, "I'm sorry. It was a rude thing to say, I was just feeling defensive."

"It's okay Sally. Don't even worry about it." Sarah said expansively as she watched Sally drop the couch into its bed position. Sally got Sarah a pillow and blanket and said goodnight and went off to bed pointing out the bathroom on her way.

Sarah lay down and was instantly and soundly asleep.

Chapter 6

Jo kept looking at her watch willing the hands to go around faster. She was going out of her mind wanting to know if Sarah had left or stayed. If she had thought about those kisses once, she had thought about them a hundred, a thousand times. "This will never do." she thought to herself "This will never do." She had made her purchase and gone straight back to the airport and caught the next fight home. The entire plane trip Jo tossed in her business class seat and dreamed of Sarah's soft lips, Jo was having trouble controlling her excitement as the plane rolled to a stop and she got her only bag from the overhead compartment. She strode quickly out of the airport, having passed through customs in New York, got into her truck and headed off up the highway with thoughts of Sarah's softness rolling through her mind. "Maybe I can catch her on her morning run again." she thought with amused excitement. Even with Melissa, there had not been this giddy feeling. Her excitement dimmed for a while as she thought about Melissa, but unavoidably her mind went back to Sarah and began whirling again.

Once she got to the house, Jo tried to look casual as she hurried up to Sarah's room taking the steps two at a time. She tapped softly and went in only to find the room empty, and the bed made. Her heart aching she thought "She's left" as she walked into the bathroom, but there was all of her things lined up in a row by the mirror. "She hasn't left. But where is she?" Jo wondered at a loss. Shrugging and disappointed she went down the east hall to her room and unpacked, changed into her usual jeans, boots and a T-shirt, and headed out to talk to Sam with her precious cargo from Germany.

"So, you're back early Jo." Sam said surprised to see her. A strange look drifted across his face and then he looked very casual again.

"Yea, I figured there was no reason to hang around over there and caught an early flight back." Jo replied trying to sound as casual as Sam looked. "Have you seen Sarah today? I was wondering how she was doing."

"Well, now that you mention it, last time I saw her, she was headed into town last night to meet up with your friend Sally." Sam said trying to make it sound like it wasn't anything.

Jo's eyes flared and turned into liquid fire, "Oh she did, did she?" she replied "Well, I hope she had a fun time with old Sally."

Sam couldn't miss the jealousy in Jo's voice and wondered at it. This was the first time in a long time that Jo had shown any interest in anyone. With one eyebrow slowly sliding up his face he kept his tone neutral as he said "I expect that she would. Sally is a nice enough lady."

Jo turned without replying, hearing the sound of a vehicle approaching and saw one of the Jeeps coming to a stop next to her truck in front of the main house. She quietly watched Sarah as she climbed out of the Jeep looking down right radiant as she looked around and then went inside. "Yea, she looks like she had a great time all right." She grumbled under her breath. Sam remained silent, his eyes glancing from where Sarah had been and back again to Jo in an amused way. Jo abruptly suggested that they go out to the pasture and look over the new brands to make sure none of them had become infected.

Sam agreed affably "Okay, Jo, but give me about an hour to finish up this paperwork."

"Okay, Sam" Jo said glancing at her watch "See you in an hour."

Sarah looked everywhere for Jo before going up to her room. She had seen her truck from the highway and couldn't wait to see her. But Jo was no where to be found so she decided on a bath to get the bar smell off of her skin and then fresh clothes. Once in her room she stripped, filled the bath and buzzed Maria who showed up a short time later. "Maria, could you bring me a cup of coffee, please. I know you are busy, if it's too much to ask, I'll get it."

"Oh, no you caught me in a quiet time. Sure I'll get you one dear. You look almost as bad as Jo does when she's been out on the town. Did you have a nice time last night?" Maria queried in a friendly tone "The coffee might take a little while because I'm going to make a fresh pot," she added.

"I really did, Maria. I had a lot of fun. Thanks for asking. And thanks for getting me the coffee, no hurry." Sarah answered from the bathroom. She heard the door close as Maria went out.

A little while later there was a short rap on the door and it opened and closed, assuming it was Maria, Sarah said "That was really fast Maria, just set it down by the bed and I'll drink it when I get out."

There was no reply and Sarah turned to find Jo standing in the door of her bathroom looking down at her through dark fiery eyes. Sarah gasped, not realizing there would be anyone standing there, much less Jo. Unable to reach a towel or her robe without coming out of the water Sarah just sat there, unsure of what those dangerous eyes meant and what to do about it, she breathed "Jo" making Jo's heart beat double time. Sarah's startled emerald green eyes melted and completely opened to Jo's "I'm so glad to see you." And as she relaxed she added ruefully, "When you left you didn't mention that you were going to another country and would be gone for days. I thought you were just going into town or something." She waved her arm vaguely, causing the water to ripple and her breasts to undulate.

Jo didn't answer her, in part because, she hadn't expected Sarah to be in the bathtub without a stitch on and the desire welling up in her was almost palpable, and also because she was angry with Sarah for all of the things she might have done with Sally. She knew Sarah was a very forward woman when it came to sex. "Why would Sally say no? Why should Sally say no? Why did I say no?" she thought angrily. Instead Jo just stood there in the doorway and said nothing.

Rolling so that her back was exposed and her front was not, trying to feel a little less exposed, Sarah leaned her elbows against the edge of the tub closest to Jo and said, "I went out last night to your bar and met Sally. We had a really nice time. We danced and talked and she introduced me around. I can see why you two are friends. I had a bit too much to drink though," Sarah continued under Jo's silent fiery stare, "and had to stay the night on her sofa. A miserably hard sofa, I might ad, but that's OK. I had a good time anyway." still Jo remained silent, thinking "Sally's sofa is miserably hard but... still I can't forget how she tried to pull me into her bed and seduce me, and she was still sore head to toe from that fall..."

Sarah shifted on her elbows making the small of her waist and the gentle curve from it to her hips rise briefly above to water. Jo leaned against the doorframe, wishing that Sarah would just hold still and stop all of her undulating and wiggling. It kept making her stomach flip. Finally she said, "Well, I'm glad Sally showed you a good time." her voice husky from watching Sarah and the words filled with jealousy.

Sarah immediately realized what Jo was suggesting and her soft emerald green eyes changed color to a dark fiery green. Out of the bath tub Sarah came, furious at Jo's suggestion, she forgot all about her nudity and was across the short distance standing in front of Jo dripping wet from head to toe. Then she charged Jo. "How dare you suggest that I slept with Sally. I don't even know her!" she said standing inches from Jo she shook a wet finger Jo's direction.

Stunned by the graceful fluidity of Sarah's nude, wet body and the fury in her eyes, Jo rose up to her full height and stiffened expecting a blow, but none came. Instead, there was a fire building between them as they stood there inches apart, Jo's jealousy slowly slipped away leaving only thoughts of taking Sarah in her arms and slowly making love to her. "Right here on the floor right now." she thought "I have to have this woman or I will just die." All other thoughts were gone. Sarah sensed the shift from angry suspicion to powerful passion in Jo's eyes but was still so mad at her that it didn't matter.

Their silent discussion raged on until it was interrupted by a quiet knock on the door that instantly broke the moment. As Sarah grabbed a towel, Jo turned and was across the bedroom "She is going to drive me insane, this woman is," she thought "What am I going to do with her?" passing Maria who had a cup of coffee in her hand and was looking with concern from Jo's dark smoldering eyes as she passed her on her way out the door to Sarah's fiery dark green eyes.

"Here you go." Maria said sounding casual "Nice fresh coffee. I will leave you to dress." She said looking from Sarah's furious eyes to Jo's receding back and back again and then she too was gone.

On her way out of the house Jo passed her mother's office and heard Alice call from it's interior. "When you have time Jo, I need to talk to you."

Jo thought "Great, it's never good when she needs to talk to me. So who has she found for me to marry now?" in exasperation at the thought of getting home and having two fights almost back to back she replied "Can't talk now mom, how about later. I've got to meet Sam." and out the door she went.

Sarah, her hair in a towel turban, got dressed. She picked up the still steaming cup of coffee and went out on the deck in time to watch Jo stomp over to the office in the stable. "What an insufferably difficult woman." she thought to herself but her heart wasn't in it. "Of all the nerve, thinking I would make love to her friend Sally. What kind of woman does she think I am?" Then thinking back on the morning Jo had left and how she had acted, "and for that matter just now in the bath room, coming out of the bath tub and standing there right in front of her with out a stitch on...maybe from her point of view I seem quite the hussy." Sarah sighed with frustration at this impossible situation.

Jo spent the whole day working, working really hard and thinking about nothing but the hard work she was doing. It was a trick she had learned after her father died and it had held her in good stead after the accident too. By dinner, she was feeling relaxed and in good spirits until she walked into the house. Alice called her into her office and patted the sofa next to her. "Come here and sit down for a minute, I want to talk to you Jo."

"I smell really bad, let me just take a quick shower and we'll talk after dinner." Jo suggested hopefully.

"Sit." Alice repeated and patted the sofa "and pull the doors too when you come in."

"Great," thought Jo as she closed the door and crossed the room to sit next to her mother.

"Sarah and I were talking the other day," Alice started.

Jo moved in her seat "Oh this sounds like it's going to be really bad." thought Jo unhappily.

"And" Alice continued, "I realized that I've been leaning on you very heavily, trying to make you do things that I want you to do. Instead of letting you make you own life decisions without interference. All I have ever wanted is for you to be happy, Jo. I know I'm no good at showing it but I do love you and I am very proud of you."

Jo's face showed the confusion she felt inside, this was not how she was expecting this talk to go.

"I know you are a...a...lesbian....I have known for a long time." Alice said hesitantly.

Jo's mouth fell open and then closed as she thought, "Mom has never said that word out loud, I don't even think she has ever thought that word." Alice patted Jo's hand and looked uncomfortable, "I don't understand why you are that way, but I want you to know that I accept it today, right now, as how you are. I won't try to make you date any more men. I won't meddle in your private affairs any more. I do love you and I only want you to be happy. If that is what makes you happy then so be it." there was a pause while Jo tried to understand what she was hearing from her mother and while Alice tried to figure out how to say the last piece she had to say, finally shaking her head sadly she finished, "but I will never understand Jo, never." Alice was still shaking her head as the dinner bell rang. "Well, we'll talk more about this another time, maybe" she looked at Jo's shocked face and added "or maybe not. It's up to you to bring it up now Jo." as she rose Alice added absently "Can't be late for dinner."

Jo sat there in stunned silence. Never had her mom talked to her about anything like that before. She continued to sit there in confusion about what her mom had said. Finally, she noticed that Alice was waiting for her by the door, and still sitting, she said "You talked to Sarah about this?" in disbelief.

Alice retraced her steps to where Jo still sat, "Yes dear. We talked about my hopes and dreams for you and how different they are from who you are. It really made me see how hard I have pushed you. We talked about how much I love you and how proud of you I am. We talked about how I never tell you these things. And she said that instead of me telling her, that I should tell you and so I am. I am sorry it has taken me so very long to say these things to you but now I have. Now let's go and eat dinner and not let this be between us any more. Also, I want you to start taking on more responsibility around here. I want you to start making more of the decisions so I can rest. I know you have a great head on your shoulders and it's time I take advantage of that." Alice patted Jo tenderly on the shoulder.

Jo rose in a trance and hugged her mother and said "I love you mom." And wiped the wetness from her cheeks and arm in arm they went to dinner together, a new level of understanding and acceptance between them that Jo had never thought would be possible.

As they entered the dinning hall, Jo spotted Sarah sitting in her usual place and although she wanted to talk to her, she had no idea what she would say. "Better to wait until I've had time to think before I talk to her again." she thought to herself watching Sarah animatedly tell a story to a friendly audience of work-hands. Everyone burst out laughing and Sarah laughed too. "Everyone seems to like her" she thought ruefully. "I wonder what exactly, her and mom said to each other." She thought about the times she kissed Sarah and decided that maybe, she didn't really want to know what Sarah and her mother had discussed exactly, the tops of Jo's ears burned red. She and Alice sat down in their usual places. It was one of the happiest meals that Jo and Alice had ever shared.

Jo kept trying to catch Sarah's glance, but Sarah refused to make eye contact with her. "She hates me." Jo decided half way through dinner, "she has brought about a truce, I thought would never occur and in return I accuse her of trying to steal mom's money and screwing Sally, she has good reason to hate me."

Sarah spent dinner forcing her eyes to look somewhere else besides at Jo. "She must think I'm horrible," Sarah thought to herself, "that I throw myself at everyone I meet." she couldn't even make eye contact with Jo out of a mixture of embarrassment and anger.

Towards the end of dinner Jo got up and said "It was a long trip and I'm really tired so I'm going to turn in early, night all, night Sarah." Jo saw Sarah's head jerk as she said her name "Please just look this way Sarah, please." she thought.

But Sarah didn't look, thinking that Jo was making fun of her she sat stiffly in her chair and said "night" without turning.

"Night mom" Jo added and kissed her mom's forehead.

Alice replied into Jo's ear "Good night Jo. Love you."

Jo went to her room. What she called her room was actually several connecting rooms forming a suite in the east wing. The door from the hall opened left into her office, which was where she spent most of her time. The furnishings were very simple, but comfortable consisting of a large leather sofa against a wall that was almost entirely window looking out on the formal garden, a wall filled floor to ceiling with books, and another wall half filled with books and a full wet bar built into the other half of it. Her desk was placed in the middle of the room facing the wall of books. Leading off of this room to the left past the wet bar was her bedroom proper and a large bathroom and leading off of her study to the right was a room devoted to a full sized pool table with leather pockets and a few pinball machines, she never used that room though, not any more. After looking over a few reports that had been stacked on her desk, she went over to her bar and got the bottle of Jack Daniel's and a glass. Thoughtfully she poured herself a drink, went back to her desk, kicked her boots off, unbuttoned her shirt and the top button on her jeans and put her feet up.

The only light came from her computer monitor's screen saver. She sat there in the dark worrying about her mother and wondering what she was going to do with this woman Sarah. "What can I do?" she asked herself "She does everything right and I blunder along like an idiot. But I just can't..." even as she thought, the last four words, she knew that her heart was made up for her and had been since their lips first met, "before that probably" she said to herself, swirling her drink in the glass absently. She sat there long into the night letting thoughts of Sarah roll around in her head. She remembered the first time she saw Sarah, Sarah on Lady Fire smiling, Sarah in bed after the fall, Sarah in the bathtub and out of the bathtub this afternoon, "she is going to drive me crazy." Jo thought to herself as she continued to swirl her untouched drink.

After Dinner and goodnights, Sarah went to her room. She wasn't tired, instead she was upset and confused and restless. She, desperately wanted to go to Jo and talk with her about this morning, but she felt uncertain about Jo's feeling towards her. "One moment she's looking at me with distrust and anger, the next she's kissing me until I my legs are butter. She's going to drive me crazy." Deciding that she would not go to Jo that instead Jo would have to come to her, Sarah changed and went to bed.

Chapter 7

Hours later, still awake, Sarah couldn't stand it any longer. She had to know if Jo truly loved her and wanted her the same way she wanted and loved Jo, once and for all. Throwing her matching robe on over her emerald green silk nightgown, Sarah silently barefooted her way down the hall to the east wing. She turned the corner wondering to herself "How will I know which room is hers?" She quietly opened the first door she came to on the left and looked in. The room was empty. She tried the next room and it was empty too. Getting nervous, she hesitated before reaching for the next doorknob, again she tried and again no Jo. Almost to the end of the hall now, her heart pounding at the possibility of walking into the wrong room and waking someone, she turned to go back to her room "Maybe this isn't such a good idea." She thought to herself "I can just ask her in the morning" she turned and seeing a door on the right side of the hall she decided to try one more time and opened it.

It was dark inside, but Sarah could see the light of a computer monitor shining on Jo who was deep in thought staring at a half full glass of dark liquid that she was swirling around and around. Either she hadn't noticed Sarah or was ignoring her. Sarah thinking "She must not have heard me. I wonder what she's thinking about sitting here in the dark?" quietly walked into the room and closed the door trying not to make a sound.

She slipped up to the desk and stood there just behind Jo not knowing what to say, when Jo broke the silence by saying in a low voice without turning "hello, Sarah."

Sarah came around the desk with a rustle of silk and leaned on a corner of Jo's desk. She nervously thought to herself "Here I go again, being the forward hussy that I am." and replied "Hello, I know it's late, but I couldn't sleep and I thought I would see if you were awake too and you were so I came in and..." Sarah trailed off thinking how odd this must seem to Jo having a strange woman practically throw herself at her like this. "But she probably has this happen to her all of the time...she's so very beautiful in a strong capable way."

Jo stopped swirling her drink "So you just dropped in for a friendly..." Jo paused glancing at the clock on her computer "2:17 am visit?" Jo asked with amusement glittering dangerously in her eyes. Jo's eyes slid up Sarah "Every curve under that silky fabric perfect. Leaning there on the edge of my desk in that incredible soft robe and gown, with your hair all soft and falling loose around your shoulders and face..." Jo shook her head and instantly decided she couldn't stand any more words "It is time for action, Jo. No more stopping. So far in this game of chicken you are the one that keeps flinching." Jo thought as she silently slid her fiery eyes over Sarah's beautiful slender outline in the darkness conscious of the musky sweet scent of her in the room. Silently Jo groaned wondering silently "Are you a tease Sarah or are you truly unaware of the powerful effect you have on me? Does it really matter? Either way Jo, you want her and how. It's time to find out if you are going to have a broken heart or not." she continued to watch Sarah, letting the silence stretch and build.

Unsure of what the odd tone in Jo's voice and then the silence meant Sarah shifted her weight from one foot to the other and asked nervously "Can I just turn on the light so I can see your face, Jo? Because I can't really tell what..."

Jo interrupted her words in one smooth powerful motion. Setting her untouched drink on a coaster on the desk, Jo reached out her other arm and caught Sarah around her waist and pulled her into her lap and kissed her. Sarah's mind swirled around this tender kiss trying to understand where it had come from, but gave up not wanting to think any more.

Drawing her lips away only to brush them against Sarah's temples, Jo inhaled deeply smelling Sarah's hair and the scent of her, Jo allowed herself to admit the feelings she had for Sarah. Aloud, Jo said in a dangerous husky voice filled with the promise of controlled passion "I think that our problem is we both think too much, without actually saying what our hearts feel out loud to each other...Sarah."

The way she said Sarah sent shivers of anticipation up Sarah's spine. She knew in that moment that Jo had come to some decision, but what it was she was afraid to guess at. Sarah went to reply to agree but Jo put strong fingers lightly over her mouth silencing her. Feeling the softness of Sarah's lips against her fingers, Jo groaned. Her mouth already hungered to feel those lips against her own again. Abruptly she slid her arms under Sarah and scooped her up.

Sarah grabbed Jo's neck in surprise saying, "What are you doing? Jo? Where are you taking me?" But she already knew what Jo had in mind.

Jo didn't reply but simply walked into her large bedroom with Sarah and stood her next to her massive king sized four-poster bed. Sarah watched Jo's outline as she unhurriedly stripped all of her own clothes off before approaching Sarah. Without a word Jo slowly untied Sarah's robe. Feeling the cool smooth silk against her hands, Jo sighed into Sarah's hair and slid it off of her shoulders. It slipped to the floor without protest, Sarah's heart beat wildly as she stood still, just allowing it all to happen, allowing Jo to undress her in her bedroom knowing what was going to happen next and wanting, willing it to happen. Then Jo slid her strong fingers under the shoulder straps of Sarah's nightgown. She pushed them off Sarah's shoulders and her nightgown joined the pool of green silk on the floor. Silently they stood there, inches from each other without anything on and looked at each other for a long time in the dimness, until Jo, unable to wait any longer, reached out and pulled Sarah to her.

Their lips and bodies came together in the same instant, forming a heat in Sarah like she had never known. Jo groaned and released Sarah only to find Sarah's arms still around her neck. The full body contact of this moment burned into Jo's mind. Her mouth melted against Sarah's again and then her lips began to explore Sarah's neck and shoulder, leaving a fiery trail in their wake. There was an unhurried sureness to Jo's kisses, as if they had the rest of their lives to explore each other. Sarah began burning her own trail of kisses down Jo, ready to love and fulfill this incredible woman, wanting to make Jo feel the love she had for her. Jo groaned again as Sarah began kissing her breasts, then pulled Sarah away thinking "I am in control of this moment." Jo covered Sarah's lips once again with the passionate softness of her own lips.

"Let me make love to you Sarah" Jo said softly, reluctantly releasing her. Jo pulled the sheets back and lied down on the dark blue sheets, her heart pounding at the possibility Sarah would say no and crush her heart. She thought to herself "This is the moment. I know I love her, absolutely. My heart aches for her, but does she love me? She must decide for herself." Jo left Sarah standing beside the bed to make her own mind up.

Sarah did not hesitate, knowing that more than anything in the world, she wanted this to happen.

Jo blinked back tears of relief as Sarah curled around her, their bodies colliding in passionate oblivion. Jo's kisses became less soft and more passionate. She rolled Sarah onto her back and lightly pinned her to the bed under her weight. Sarah put up no fight. Then Jo's lips began to move down Sarah's body. First her lips and tongue explored Sarah's neck and shoulders. Then Jo moved to Sarah's breasts, gently kissing around and around them until she finally reached Sarah's nipples. Sarah moaned in pleasure. She had never felt so alive under the hands and mouth of anyone before, her body responding to every caress with a powerful fiery pleasure. Jo lifted her head and powerful shoulders to look Sarah squarely in the face. In the dimness Sarah could see Jo's liquid fire eyes.

"Tell me that this is what you want, Sarah." Jo husked "Tell me that you love me. Say it out loud, Sarah."

Sarah tried to pull Jo's lips down to meet her own, but Jo would not be moved, finally Sarah responded quietly, "Yes. Yes Jo, this is what I want, more then anything. I do love you with all of my heart or I would not be here." She said softly frightened by her own admission. Then Jo replied by lowering her achingly soft lips and covering Sarah's with a deep slow kiss that moved them both to the bone. Jo kissed her way down to Sarah's breasts and kissed one, rolling her tongue slowly around and around her nipple making Sarah gasp at the electricity running down her body. Jo took each nipple, in turn until they were both hard and Sarah was softly moaning and thrashing about under her. Jo felt Sarah's slender strong fingers in her hair, demanding, trying to pull Jo's mouth up against hers again.

In no hurry and in complete steely control of herself, Jo ignored the request and continued to move down Sarah's body, from her full breasts to her firm stomach. Jo made a fiery trail. Then Jo gently parted Sarah's legs and began kissing Sarah on the insides of her thighs. Sarah groaned at the pleasure that flowed hotly over her whole body. Jo was overwhelmed by Sarah's passionate response to her and intoxicated by her sweet scent, she slowly moved back up

Sarah to kiss those lips once more. She allowed her hand to slide between Sarah's legs and feel her warm silky wet softness. "Oh, yes." thought Jo with a deep sound coming up out of her throat, "This is how it is supposed to be."

"Never before" Sarah thought through her ecstasy "never before like this" she sighed Jo's name again and again as Jo slowly, deliberately explored Sarah's silky softness, first with her fingers and then unable to resist Sarah's musky sweetness, with her mouth.

After the all-engulfing fire had consumed Sarah, she thought vaguely "It has never felt like that before, never filled me with such a sense of rightness. Never so deeply satisfying, but leaving me wanting more." as she allowed Jo to hold her tenderly. Like the legendary Phoenix bird born again from fire, Sarah felt freed and alive. With that freedom came the overwhelming need to touch Jo, to respond in kind, and show Jo the love she felt. "My turn, Jo" Sarah said quietly as she began kissing Jo.

Jo thought to herself "No...I must remain in control....I am..." she groaned with deep pleasure as Sarah's soft lips closed over one of her nipples "No one, I'm...the one...in control...no one touches me like this." Jo moaned a low desperate protest. She lay very still, trying to regain control, but still allowed Sarah's lips to make soft trails on her skin. Unwilling to stop Sarah's gentle exploration of her body, Jo silently gave in to her desire, her need for Sarah stronger then her need for control.

With a hunger Sarah didn't know she was capable of, she kissed Jo again and again exploring her body with soft demanding kisses, until Jo allowed Sarah to spread her thighs apart. Sarah tentatively began kissing Jo on her silky soft dark hair. Then with the sweet scent of Jo in her nostrils, Sarah slipped her mouth lower as a deep sob of ecstasy, escaped Jo's lips and a deep groan of pleasure came from Sarah's.

Fire spread over Jo's entire body as she let go, vaguely she thought "Never before, never before. Yes, so right, I love you Sarah."

Much later, the two of them lay entwined still kissing and caressing each other, beyond words. "I can't hold her tight enough to me." Jo thought, "I can't feel enough of her against me. I love her more then I know what to do with. What am I going to do? What am I going to do?"

Quietly Jo disengaged and said huskily "We've got to get some sleep Sarah. We've got to…" but was silenced by Sarah's tender mouth on hers. The faint brightening that comes just before dawn was in the sky when Jo's alarm clock abruptly went off. Jo lifted her head releasing Sarah's lips, unable to believe that the whole night was gone. Quietly she decided "I can afford to be late once in a while…" turned off the alarm and they continued their tender touching and kissing of each other.

What seemed like a very short time later there came a soft knock on Jo's door. A voice called in from the other room "Jo, Jo I need to talk to you right now. I'm coming in." and Sam appeared at Jo's bedroom door before either of them could move.

Sarah, Jo and Sam all looked at each other for a moment, each registering their own reaction to the surprise interruption, before Sam spoke.

He silently assessed the situation, one eyebrow slowly rising up in surprise and approval and said in a neutral business like tone addressing the two of them "Jo…Sarah…sorry if I'm interrupting," then his attention went to Jo alone "Jo, your mother's very ill. An ambulance is on its way, but she's asked for you. You better go right now." and he was gone knowing Jo would be at her mother's side in moments.

"Damn, damn, damn. Doc. Peterson was afraid of this." Jo said throwing back the covers and striding across the room. Jo grabbed the nearest clothes and put them on and, glancing briefly at Sarah and then away once again stunned by Sarah's beauty and said "You better get dressed too, Sarah." and she was gone.

Sarah put her nightgown and bathrobe on and slipped through the hall passed several people to her room trying to be as casual as she could under the circumstances. She quickly dressed and stood leaning against the counter in her bathroom looking at her reflection. Smelling Jo's scent on her, Sarah quietly got a washcloth and washed her face and then her hands. Looking back in the mirror she saw the confusion that showed in her eyes, a deep conflict between wanting Jo and worry about Alice. She brushed her hair smooth and went out into the storm of the hall.

Chapter 8

"Mom, mom how are you doing?" Jo asked as she sat down on the edge of Alice's bed, deep concern intertwined with fear in her dark eyes as she leaned over her mother.

"Jo, it's time." Alice whispered and said nothing else for a while. She just looked at her daughter with a deep love and a new understanding shining in her eyes. "Grandbabies would have been nice, but that's okay. Jo try to be happy, promise me that you'll be happy. You and Sarah both." Alice pleaded in a strong whisper.

Jo took her mother's hand in hers and said nothing. Shocked by her words and knowing what Alice meant by 'It's time' she finally said "It's not time yet, look at you, you look fine to me." and patting her mother's hand, she repeated "you look just fine." Jo blinked rapidly.

Alice repeated in an urgent and intense whisper that brought her up out of the bed a little "Promise me Jo. Promise me that you'll be happy."

Jo looked at the intensity on her mother's face and knowing how much effort these words were costing her said "I promise, mom, but you're going to be just fine, you'll see. Just rest for now okay?"

Alice seemed satisfied and lay heavily back into her bed whispering faintly "Remember your promise Jo, don't forget." and said nothing more while they waited for the ambulance to arrive.

The paramedics arrived moments later. Deep concern was etched on their faces as they gently moved her onto a gurney and whisked her away to the hospital. She was admitted and immediately moved to the Intensive Care Unit. At first she was whispering little, urgent last minute commands, but after only a few hours she stopped talking all together and by evening she had slipped into a coma. Doc. Peterson came by and said it was massive heart failure and the prognosis was dismal. Jo never left her side, never let go of her hand.

Sarah wandered the institution gray halls of the hospital, waiting and not knowing what was going on, ICU only allowed immediate family in. Worry consumed her. "Would Alice be okay? Would Jo be okay? Why didn't anyone tell her anything?" she wondered. Finally she saw Sally and hurried over to her, glad to see someone she knew. "Sally is she okay? Is Alice going to be okay? What happened to her?"

Sally looked at her with a deep compassion that said more then words and replied "Honey, Alice is dying."

Sarah's eyes went wide "What? What? Alice? Alice is dying? But..." Sarah hunted for something to pin this information too. She looked around, went over to a chair and sat down. Sally quietly followed her understanding grief and shock when she saw it.

"She is moving on. We all knew it was coming, but didn't know when." Sally shook her head sadly. "Her poor little heart is just worn out and there is nothing left that can be done. This is it."

Sarah looked stunned "I had no idea. She never told me. I...we..." she trailed off. Her mind jumped around from shock. Absently thinking about last night she asked, "How is Jo?"

Sally turned and looked at Sarah closely. She had her suspicions about what had been happening between Jo and Sarah. Jo had been too casual when asking about her night out with Sarah when they had talked yesterday evening, but now she knew with absolute certainty and approved "It's about time Jo let someone into her life again." she thought to herself. She replied casually "She knew this was coming too, but Alice is her mother. She'll take it hard I guess. Jo's sort of an all or nothing type of person." She quietly watched Sarah take this in.

"I could be there for her. I could help her through this if she would let me, Sally." Sarah said quietly.

Sally recalled the way Jo was after the accident and seriously doubted that she would accept comforting from anyone including Sarah. But instead of saying that, she changed the subject, saying instead "Hey, let's not loose touch when you go back to Houston." and pulled out her wallet and got a card out "Here, this has my home number, work number, and email address on it. Call any time. If you want to know how things are going, or just gab, give me a holler or drop a line, Sarah. You're good people and Jo needs you, even if she won't admit it right now."

Sarah blinked at Sally and took the card not sure what Sally meant. She stammered "I...I don't know what you're talking about Sally, but thanks, I'd love to stay in touch with you." She smiled trying to regain her composure, wondering, "What has Jo told her?"

Sally winked at her in a friendly way and said "Okay Sarah, what ever you say. Gotta get back upstairs." and left her sitting in the waiting room.

Sarah flipped the card over and over in her fingers thinking about the things Sally had said and the fact that soon, very soon, she would be going back to Houston, and Jo would not and her friend, Alice, was dying and she hadn't even known that she was ill, while tears of sadness and confusion rolled unchecked down her cheeks.

"What a great big terrible mess this is." she thought wiping at her cheek. My best friend is dying and I've fallen hopelessly in love with her daughter. My crying heart is flying away with me." She sat in the waiting room late into the night.

It was a small room with a few struggling potted plants in the corners, clinging to life under fluorescent lights, a coffee table with magazines so old no one wanted them enough to steal them and uncomfortable chairs with bright yellow vinyl seats perhaps left over from the seventies. There was a phone in one corner that would occasionally ring and a TV hanging in one of the corners by the ceiling and an insufferable clock slowly ticking the seconds away hour by hour on the wall. Sam checked on her from time to time and let her know what was happening, "Probably Sally said something to him." she thought appreciatively.

Abruptly at nearly four in the morning, Jo came in to the room where Sarah was sitting and without looking at her stiffly said "She's gone." and walked out again leaving Sarah more alone then she had ever been.

It took all of Jo's control to say those two words and not break down in front of Sarah. Not able to stay one moment longer and not able to explain, Jo headed out into the darkness to her truck where she could grieve alone "So soon." Jo thought "I've got too much to sort out. We had just begun talking, just begun getting to know each other. My mother...gone." She pounded her steering wheel in hurt frustration, inconsolable in her grief.

Sarah blinked back tears, but they slid out the sides of her eyes anyway and rolled down her cheeks. She dropped her face into her hands and cried in big gasping sobs, oblivious to everything around her. Not knowing or caring if the tears were for Alice or for herself, her friend was dead and Jo, after last night, obviously didn't want her any more. The agony of Jo's rejection was almost as bad as that from Alice's death.

Sam shifted uncomfortably in front of Sarah waiting for her to notice him. Finally deciding he'd better interrupt he said "Sarah, here," and handed her a tissue "let me take you home." She looked up at him through puffy bloodshot eyes and accepted the offered tissue without a word. She dabbed at her eyes and started to cry again, but followed him out of the hospital and into his truck.

He was silent all the way back to the ranch unaccustomed to such open raw grief and not knowing quite how to react. "Poor girl." he thought knowing how much the correspondence between Alice and Sarah had meant to Alice, he suspected that it meant a lot to Sarah too and then there was Jo. He sighed, knowing that she had already headed out to her cabin on the other side of the ranch with word that she was not to be disturbed by anyone for any reason, except the funeral time, for a while. Leaving Sarah to her grief Sam just drove and thought "Sarah's just not gonna understand."

Lost in her own thoughts, Sarah didn't break the silence either except with an occasional sniffle. She felt she had just been hit with a one, two punch with Alice's death and Jo's rejection. Once back at the ranch, she went up the stairs pausing at the top trying to decide if she should go to Jo's room or her own.

Sam watched her hesitation from below with sad eyes, "She's good people." he thought, "Jo couldn't do better." shaking his head sadly, knowing what she would find in Jo's room. "They'll either work it out or they won't, nothing I can explain or help with though." he thought as he sighed heavy hearted, turned and walked towards the kitchen.

Finally, she turned towards Jo's room, her instinct to comfort Jo stronger then her fear of rejection. She walked down the hall. Her insides shaking, she stopped outside Jo's door. Finally she took a deep breath and opened the door, the room was dark just like last night but Jo's office was empty. She wandered into Jo's bedroom thinking that maybe she would be in there, but it was empty too. Silently she sat down on the edge of the bed remembering the night before and confusion threatened to drown her. "I just don't understand…I just don't understand." her heart wailed in mournful agony. "What we have is so good, so perfect. Why isn't it enough for Jo? I could be there for her if she wanted me. Where is she?" Quietly she rose and returned to her own room, her world falling apart around her.

She cried silently, "What am I going to do? I can't just go back. I can't just leave Jo without at least talking to her first. Where in the world is she?"

Chapter 9

A day went by and Sarah had no one to talk to since Alice was gone and Jo was not to be found. With resignation she wandered the grounds and through the house in silent grief. The afternoon found her standing in front of the door to Jo's empty room again. She went in and listlessly poked around. In the night stand next to Jo's bed she ran across a color photo in a small silver frame of Jo with a woman. They were arm in arm and smiling. With a start, Sarah realized that the other woman in the photograph must be or must have been Jo's lover at one time. She was very curvy and had curly blond hair that went to the nap of her neck. This mysterious woman had a wonderful mischievous smile and pale blue dancing eyes. Her curiosity aroused Sarah looked around some more, but that was the only picture she found of her. She put it back where she had found it feeling guilty for invading Jo's privacy and went back to her own room.

She silently took her sketch pad out onto the deck with her and sketched her impressions of the last few days in powerful abstract images, letting her emotions flow out and onto page after page, tears running down her face unnoticed. After dinner running across the card that Sally had given her she decided to give her new friend a call and see what she was doing. She went down to the office and sat down on the visitor's chair unwilling to sit in Alice's old chair and dialed the number for home on the card.

"Hello." came the familiar voice from the other end of the phone.

"Hey, Sally, it's Sarah. What are you doing tonight?" she asked.

"Oh, don't have anything really planned, exactly. Why don't you come over and I'll pop some pop corn and we can watch movies?" Sally suggested.

"That sounds great. I'll be over then in a little while. I've got to get out of this house for a bit."

"Okay, sweetie, when ever. I'll be here." and with that they hung up.

Sarah borrowed the jeep and went into town, the cool air on her face felt refreshing to her. Once she got to Sally's house, they started talking and never did watch any movies. Instead they talked about Alice and her condition and Jo and finally about her feelings for Jo.

Abruptly Sally decided that Sarah should know about the accident, had a right to know. "Sarah there is something I'm going to tell you about, and it's bad." Sarah not knowing what to think just listened quietly. "Let's see, must have been three years ago last September, Jo and Melissa were out riding in the mountains."

Sarah interrupted "Melissa? Is she blond and real pretty?"

Sally looked at Sarah with surprise "Yes she was." The 'was' silenced any more questions that Sarah had. Sally paused waiting to see if Sarah was going to ask anything else, then continued. "They used to go on horse back trips that would take them high into those mountains and this trip was no different then a dozen others they had taken. They would go up to the meadows and camp out sometimes for several days, fish in the stream and who knows what,"

Sally sighed, "but this time while they were way up there Melissa's horse slipped on the path, probably loose rock or something and went sliding down the mountain side with her. Jo couldn't get to her for a long time, because she had slid a long ways down into a ravine. By the time she got there Melissa was dead. Horse died too."

A flash of understanding came into Sarah's eyes as she remembered her horse incident and the fear in Jo's eyes afterward.

"Jo stayed with Melissa's body until someone went looking for them a few days later, wouldn't leave her side and couldn't get her up to the path by herself, though she tried countless times, she didn't have a cell phone yet, so she just waited. She felt certain that somehow it was her fault that horse slipped, I think. Maybe she felt that if she had gotten to Melissa faster she could have saved her somehow, I don't know. But for the last three years Jo has not even looked at anyone, until you came along that is." Sally smiled and patted her shoulder. "But the problem, as I see it now, is timing. You see honey, Jo's got to say good bye to her mother now, and the way she grieves is she goes off by herself for a while, sometimes a long while, and doesn't talk to anyone much until she can face the world again." Sarah's eyes showed her devastation but Sally continued. "Now I know that she loves you Sarah, because Jo is just not a fly by night casual sort of person, but I also know that right now, it probably doesn't feel like it. You're gonna have to give Jo some time, woman. Jo's complicated, but when she gives her heart away she means it. Just give her some time."

Sarah looked doubtful, "I don't know what to think Sally. I don't know if she loves me or not. One minute she is, well, I mean, one minute I think she does, and then the next minute she does something and I'm not sure any more. All I know is that in the last week my friend has died and I have fallen head over heals in love with her daughter who won't talk to me." she hung her head and unwelcome tears slid down her face again. "You know Sally you are the only person who seems at all sane today." Sarah added, through her tears.

Sally handed her a tissue and sat down on the futon next to her "Oh, honey, I didn't mean to make you cry. Alice lived a good life. You should be glad you knew her, she was a wonderful lady and wouldn't want you shedding tears over her. Why she'd say, 'get on with it.' life is passing you by, no tears for me. And Jo, she just has her own way of dealing with her grief. She'll come back to you, just give it time."

Sarah looked at Sally through her tears "But I don't have time, I'm going back to Houston the day after the funeral first thing in the morning. That is the longest I could put going back off. I've got an art opening that evening and I have to be there."

Sally clicked her tongue at Sarah and replied trying to sound cheerful "Well, now you can always come back and visit old Sally if you want. I have this wonderful sofa for sleeping on. Who knows what will happen tomorrow."

Sarah thought about this for a while and said after some time "You know Sally, I really would enjoy coming up to visit you. Even if Jo and I don't work out, Montana is absolutely beautiful and you have kept me sane I think."

Sally looked pleased "Well the futon is almost always available, unless some drunken friend is crashed out on it," she chuckled as she nudged Sarah in a friendly way.

Sarah laughed too, her mood lifting somewhat. Against Sally's wishes, Sarah went back to the ranch, in part for the drive and in part hoping Jo would appear. Once back she went up to her room and slept soundly out of shear exhaustion buffered with a little hope for the first time in days, even though Jo was still no where to be found.

The next afternoon Sarah spent a long time getting ready. She took the time to mentally brace herself for what was going to happen in a few hours. The wake for Alice would begin soon. Most of Alice's family and friends had either driven or flown in, over the last two days, and more would get here tonight. The funeral was tomorrow, but it seemed to be flying up on Sarah with agonizing slowness. Still, there had been no sign of Jo. "Where was she?" Sarah wondered, "People just don't fall off of the planet like that." But everyone she asked had no idea where Jo had tucked herself away. Sarah suspected that they knew but just were not telling.

After her shower, Sarah went through her clothes to see if she had anything appropriate for a wake and a funeral. The closest thing she had was her black jeans and a dark charcoal gray top she had intended to wear home. It didn't look formal enough for a funeral but it would have to do. She dried her heavy brown hair, pulled it up, piled it on top of her head and pinned it down here and there into a more formal hairdo. "At least being flat broke for all those years taught me something." She thought as she looked in the mirror and absently patted a few loose strands into place. "I can make my hair do just about anything. Alice would be proud." Sarah sighed despondently and pulled her clothes on. Thinking about Jo's strong, gentle hands and soft lips on her skin, she sighed again. "Well, she's got to show up sometime. Maybe she'll be at the wake." Sarah thought to herself absently. "I wonder what she'll wear."

Out of excuses, she headed down the stairs to the dining room to see if she could be helpful. The room was completely rearranged for the wake, with all of the chairs moved into small groups around to the edge of the room, the table was obviously going to be set up like a buffet. Maria immediately put her to work laying out the spread on the table. Sarah obediently helped move bowls and platters of food onto the table and silverware and plates into stacks on the end. She helped get trash cans set up in convenient places, set up the large coffee pot and got all of the coffee cups out and next to it. She found the sugar and creamer set and got it filled and out too along with some spoons. In short order the dinning room looked like it was ready. Sarah got herself a cup of coffee leaned against the wall and watched Maria, puffy-eyed, work in the kitchen, wondering how this was going to go. "Maria, is some one going to speak? I've never been to a wake."

Maria looked at Sarah in disbelief and said, "You've never been to a wake?" Sarah shook her head 'no' "Well, a wake is like a great big party given in honor of the person who passed. People are supposed to be happy and share happy memories about them. Sometimes people pass photos around and tell stories. Alice made all of her own arrangements before she died, even down to the list of people invited to the wake and funeral and what to serve. She's like that though, so very organized. I will miss her." Maria shook her head sadly, while her hands continued their motion without pause. "You should try to enjoy yourself tonight. It's what Alice wants," she added looking at Sarah closely "Just let things happen and try to enjoy the evening. Alice has wonderful friends."

Sarah wondered at Maria using the present tense thinking, "It must have been a slip. I'm sure she meant to use past tense, now that Alice is gone. And how could Alice still have friends? Must have been a mistake." Sarah picked out a good spot to people watch and settled in for the night as people began arriving. The first thing she noticed was the wide diversity of people that were scattered about the room. Old and young, wealthy and working class, women and men, there were people from every walk of life and every ethnicity surrounding her and they were all united in their sadness at the loss of Alice. "Some party", Sarah thought gloomily as she watched subdued people drift in and out of quiet conversation groups. Occasionally a few people would laugh softly, but over all a very subdued group of about a hundred people.

Sam quietly sidled up to Sarah and asked, "What time do you leave in the morning, Sarah?" startling her.

With a small jump she replied "Oh! Sam, I didn't hear you come up beside me. I've delayed my departure one day so I could stay for the funeral. I guess I should have told you, I'm sorry. I've just been in my own world since Alice died. I just had no idea she was even sick..." she trailed off into silence.

Sam's eyes reflected a deep understanding, as he said "Well, don't worry about it, Sarah. I'm glad you're staying another day," and he quietly patted her shoulder. "Just let me know when you need that ride to the airport and I'll make sure you make your flight," he said before wandering off to greet a couple that had just walked in.

Sarah wondered nervously if he suspected that her strongest reason for attending the funeral, something she never did, hating funerals, was the faint hope of talking to Jo one last time before leaving.

Feeling a sudden need to be outside, away from the press of strangers, she excused herself saying that she wasn't feeling well, and was going to lie down and left. Once outside, in the crystal stillness of the night, she wandered over to the corral to watch the horses. Unaware of a pair of dark eyes silently watching her from the shadows, she looked for Lady Fire, the horse that had thrown her, but couldn't find her in the group. She did spot Chester though and called to him, "Chester, come here boy, here Chester Cheetos." and clicked her tongue. Chester's big coffin head came up and he watched her from a distance trying to decide if maybe he should go over to her or not. He finally decided that maybe he would investigate on the off chance there was a little nibble of food involved and wandered over towards her at a slow plodding stroll. Stopping out of reach he smelled the air "In search of food," Sarah thought to herself, and finding none he quietly turned and walked back over to where he had been, nonchalantly leaving his back to her, ending any further possibility for discussion.

Sarah sighed and walked along the fence towards the stables tapping her fingers on each fence post as she went. She walked passed the stables oblivious to the eyes that followed her every move, as she passed the jeeps and headed out towards the watering hole.

Jo's curiosity was aroused as she watched Sarah wander around the pump house toward the dock and she wondered to herself "What can she possibly be doing out here? The wake is still going on. Why isn't she inside?" She silently followed Sarah keeping well in the shadows and watched.

Sarah quietly walked out onto the little landing that she now knew was there at the watering hole for swimmers, nude or not, and sat down and then laid down stretching out with her head toward the water and rolled onto her tummy, trailing her hand in the water off of the end of the dock and staring at the dark, liquid surface. She remembered with clear focus the moment Jo already stripped of her clothes, walked out here and dived into the water. She remembered the moonlight on her dark rough hair and her marble smooth body, the way her breasts rested round and firm on her chest muscles, her back and powerful shoulders, her slender waist and hips, and she absently traced outlines in the water. She watched the ripples roll out from the lines onto the still, dark midnight water and as tears began to fall freely creating their own ripple pattern, she buried her head in her arm and sobbed into the night. After a long while she rolled over onto her back to look at the blurry sky in absolute misery. "Oh, Alice why did you have to die? Why didn't you tell me that you were sick at least?" Sarah asked the sky. "Jo, where are you?"

Jo leaned against the stables and stared at Sarah's soft form stretched out on the landing in open invitation, wondering at her. "I know she doesn't know I'm watching her, but the way she moves. Everything she does, it's as if she was teasing me, taunting me with her gentle inviting softness," a deep pain lanced through Jo as Sarah's sobs suddenly broke the stillness of the moment. Jo turned her face into her arm. "I can't watch her cry like that. My mother is gone, and Sarah..." She thought to herself "She is going to kill me. I don't know what to do. I want to love her and hold her forever and I just want her to leave and never come back so I won't have to see or feel her gentleness again. It all hurts so much. Ah, Melissa, how could I have let you die like that. There was just nothing I could have done. You know that don't you. Oh God, I'm so sorry. But it was three years ago Melissa, three years. Maybe it is time to move on, like Sally says. Maybe Sally's right. It has been three years." Jo silently pounded the side of the barn refusing to let the tears come that burned in her throat and the corners of her eyes. "It was a mistake to come up here. I can't, deal with this right now, maybe...later," she thought and she slipped away leaving Sarah, still alone on the end of the landing with her own thoughts of Jo, unaware of how close they had been.

After a long time Sarah's tears stopped rolling down her face into her ears and she dried her eyes and sat up into a small compressed ball. Her arms hugging her legs close, her chin resting on her knees, she quietly promised herself "Whether I talk to Jo tomorrow at the funeral or not, when I get back to Houston, I'm going to call Barb and Jodi up and ask them to take me out on the town with them. There must be someone out there for me, and if it isn't Jo then it is another woman," but she knew even as she said this promise softly out loud that it was going to be a while before she was over Jo, if she ever did get completely over her. She straightened her shoulders a little "No." she said aloud. "I am going to do that. No more thinking about what ifs," but her mind was on the funeral. "One last chance Jo, one last chance..." Stiffly, Sarah got up and stretched the left over cricks out of her muscles before heading upstairs to bed. Emotionally exhausted, she slept soundly after her quiet promise under the big Montana sky.

Chapter 10

Sarah awoke the morning of the funeral to the alarm clock. She rubbed her sore eyes and looked around the gloomy room then back at the alarm clock verifying the time. "Usually by now the sun is shining in the French doors a little." she thought as she dragged out of bed. Everything seemed so quiet that she found herself creeping over to the window as quietly as she could to not disturb the silence. She pulled one of the gossamer curtains aside and looked out on a cold bleak day.

Opening the door she discovered that the temperature had dropped sharply in the night and as the wind blew at her thin silk nightgown she shivered and shut the door. "Great." she thought morosely to herself "The only coat I have is a bright neon green. If I don't wear it I'll just freeze and if I do wear it I'll look like the only jolly leprechaun at the funeral." She walked over to the closet and got her coat out and held it up, it was just as bright as she had remembered it. She broke the silence by saying aloud "I'm sorry Alice, but if I don't wear it I'll freeze. I hope you don't mind." nobody answered, not that she expected anyone to, but she did feel a warmth around her briefly. She shook her head astounded at herself,

"You sure are suggestible Sarah, now, the heater probably just came on is all. Go and take your shower." but she decided on taking advantage of the tub one last time before her flight in the morning. "Okay, just two more times, once this morning and once when we get back, or maybe after supper." she thought to herself, feeling guilty for indulging herself like that. "I just love this tub." she sighed as she sank into the warm waters allowing her head to go beneath the surface, wetting her hair into long slick ribbons.

When her hair was wet it hung all the way to her waist. She reached for the shampoo and lathered her hair into a foamy crown. She quietly played with her hair, discovering that if she stood up she could see the top of her head in the mirror. So she spent a while rearranging her hair into crazy shapes and laughing at them. "It feels so good to laugh," she thought, feeling better and not really knowing why.

She sobered up and rinsed her hair and rolled it into a towel. Then she leaned back and day dreamed about Jo and her living happily ever after, "If only it really happened like in the movies, I would turn around in slow motion" she said as she began to turn towards the door as a silent, desperate hope filled her heart "and Jo would be standing there watching me like the other day, leaning against the door frame, just watching me with those wonderful unfathomable dark eyes of hers." but even before she got all the way turned towards the door she knew Jo would not be there. "Oh well, can't punish a woman for wishing." she said aloud her heart aching.

She finished soaking in the tub and climbed out, the shine of the water making her skin seem slippery. She quietly inspected her trim, fit frame in the mirror. "I could be one of those aerobics instructors on TV." she said turning from side to side. "I am smart, pretty, and a talented artist too. Surely I will be able to find someone else." her eyes reflected the hopelessness she felt even as she tried to sound upbeat. "Alice will help me find someone. Won't you Alice?" she asked aloud, trying to sound light as her heart cried at the loss of Alice and Jo. She dried off her body and began the long process of getting her thick mane of hair completely dry. After it was nearly dry, she put the hot curlers in, glad that she had brought them after all.

Reassessing her outfit for the funeral, she decided on her emerald green sweater and black jeans instead, "Since I'll be in a bright coat there is no reason to wear that little top and the sweater will be much warmer. I wonder how long the service will be." she said quietly chatting with herself. As she waited for her curlers to cool, she dressed and opened the door again to let the cool air swirl around her. "This really is good funeral weather, Alice. You couldn't have done a better job if you had ordered it, but then again maybe you did. Maria said you planned the whole thing. I would not expect you to overlook something as important as the weather." Sarah said aloud in a conspiratorial voice once again breaking the silence. Sarah unrolled her hair and fluffed it out into soft curls with her fingers. A firm hater of hair spray she would not use it. She had decided to leave it down today so she was finished.

She looked around the room and realizing that she had stuff spread all over the place, decided that after lunch she would pack everything up except what she would need for her trip home that afternoon. "That way I won't have to do it the last minute, when I'll be in a hurry," she thought as she went out the door. With only a brief pause at the top of the stairs and a quick glance towards Jo's room, she went on to the dining room in search of some coffee and maybe a little nibble of something "since there will be no morning run today either" she sighed and shook her head. "I have been so bad, where is my discipline I ask you?" she said to herself raising Maria's eyebrow as they joined up in the foyer, and headed the same way.

"Ah, so now we are both talking to ourselves." Maria said to her with a friendly sad smile. "Only just this morning, I was saying to myself that I really shouldn't talk to myself out loud so much or people will start to think things, and here you are talking away to yourself too. It makes me feel better to know that I am not alone in my private talking." Maria chuckled quietly as they walked together.

Sarah smiled as she put her coat on a chair in the dining room "Ah, Maria, it is a bad habit. Maybe we are already crazy and don't know it and the talking to ourselves aloud is just a symptom." Sarah said chuckling. "Maybe," Maria replied and handed her a cup of coffee before she could ask for one.

"Thanks." Sarah said indicating the coffee and gratefully retreated back into silence, as she looked out over the garden and the field beyond shrouded in gray gloomy mist. "What a yucky day." she thought as she sipped her coffee.

Her thoughts were interrupted by Maria "Breakfast is going to be in a little while, work has been canceled today and everyone needed extra time to get ready so do you want to join us?" Maria asked.

"Sure, that would be really nice. Thanks for asking." Sarah answered and then realizing that Maria was waiting for her to offer to help asked, "Do you need any help?"

"Oh yes, that would be very nice, since Rosa is getting ready today. Alice was like her grandmother. She is very sad." Maria answered handing Sarah big piles of plates through the door.

Sarah carefully set the table and thought "This house will be so different without Alice around. It will be so much quieter." Suddenly a burst of noise greeted her as the work hands began to come into the room. They were laughing and cutting up, the only visible difference to Sarah was they had on their Sunday best clothes and they were clean. "Well, maybe not much quieter after all." she thought to herself. A large group gathered, ate put their dishes in the kitchen and was gone in about thirty minutes.

Having consumed three platters of scrambled eggs two loaves of toasted bread two platters of bacon and one of ham slices and who really knows how much coffee, they left the room to silence again. Sarah quietly wiped the table off amazed at the amount of food they ate. "Maria? How do you keep them fed?" she asked while she wiped.

Maria laughed "It is quite a job, just keeping food in the house to cook and then getting it all cooked to be ready at the same time, but I have a secret. Come here and I'll show you," Sarah walked into the kitchen where Maria stood. "See?" Maria asked as she held an enormous walk in freezer open "and see?" she asked again as she opened another door into a walk in refrigerator "and see what a beautiful stove and oven I have? It is state of the art. Alice got it for me, said I could pick anything out I wanted for the kitchen anything at all, if it meant I could keep everyone fed. So it isn't as hard as it looks from out there." she chuckled.

Sarah looked dubious "I couldn't do it." she said with absolute certainty.

"Ah, well, you get used to it after a while. It's not that hard." Maria looked over at Sarah and burst out laughing at the look of sincere doubt on Sarah's face. "Well, maybe it takes a little practice." she finally admitted lightly. "Why don't you ride with us to the funeral, there is room, then you won't have to drive alone all that way." Sarah, who had not even thought about how she would get to and from the funeral accepted immediately. "Good I'll just finish up here, then check on the lunch stuff and round everyone up and we'll be ready to get started over there."

"Is it very far then?" Sarah asked remembering that Maria had three kids at the ranch and three more children somewhere else, thinking maybe she should drive herself after all.

"Well, it's far to walk to today because I think it might rain. You know Alice's body was cremated." Maria said looking at Sarah for confirmation, Sarah nodded silently, "Well, she requested that they bury her ashes in the family plot next to her husband. I guess they have already done that too. We are just sort of going up there to send her off. She has a picture sitting up there where her ashes are and little notes for everyone that Sam has been assigned to hand out."

Apprehension prickled Sarah's neck, "Alice wrote me a note to be read after her death? What in the world would she have written me that she couldn't tell me in person?"

Maria noticed Sarah's odd look and said "The notes are private, Sam is just handing them out, not reading them out loud. There is a short thing Alice wrote maybe a page long that Sam is going to read out loud first." Maria paused while she cut several sandwiches in half at once with a large knife, "I guess after they are all handed out everyone will probably go home and read them in their own time. I'm sure that some people will read theirs up on the hill and stand around there for a while, although Alice isn't up there."

Sarah watched Maria curiously thinking "That is the second time she has talked of Alice in the present tense as if she is still living and walking around here." but instead of mentioning this, said aloud, "So what time are we all heading up there?"

"Oh, I figure we'll all troop up there in about an hour or so." Maria said after a short pause while she cut up more sandwiches.

"Okay then, I'll meet you on the front porch then in about an hour." Sarah suggested.

Maria's face softened as she looked at Sarah's sad puffy face, "Sounds fine dear." she said as her hands kept moving.

Sarah turned and slipped away down the silent hall in search of something to do for the next hour. "Guess I'll walk around the garden" she thought to herself tossing around for something to keep her mind busy. Turning along the stairs, she headed out the French doors she had noticed there and walked out into the cold blustery weather. She quietly wandered through the garden inspecting the nameplates on all of the plants neatly printed in indelible marker on a dull metal surface. Nearly every plant had one. After a short time Sarah realized that Alice had probably written all of those little tags, along with each plants watering and fertilizing schedule and sunlight needs, knowing that her life was coming to an end and wanting to pass on the information to someone. Probably Sam or maybe Maria or one of their children would take care of the garden now. A tear ran down her cheek knowing that gardening was probably not on Jo's list of things she would do. Idly she wondered how Jo was and what she was up to. She had seemed so cold to her at the hospital so distant. Maybe she had gone off to some other country to buy more sperm or something. It had not seemed like Jo and Alice were very close or anything. Silently she ran her fingers along the back of a wrought iron park bench and then sat down on the hard wooden slats that made up the seat, absently brushing her hair back out of her face.

Suddenly, Maria came flying out of the dining room and broke her thoughts with strong scolding. "Now, Sarah you get right back in that house and go put on a coat, it is much to cold for you out here right now!" her finger waving in the air in her direction.

Sarah realizing the sting of the wind on her face, and that Maria was right, replied "Okay Maria, I'm heading in now." as she rose and walked back into the house through the French doors she had entered the garden from. Once inside Sarah realized just how cold she was, and headed back upstairs to see if maybe she had anything warmer to wear. "Maybe a T-shirt under the sweater" she thought to herself. She went upstairs and added another layer of clothing under her outfit and gloves she found in a drawer. A scarf and hat was added from the drawer over the top of her very cold ears. "Thank goodness this guest room came fully stocked with a drawer of hats, scarves mittens and gloves to accessorize with for those of us who do not even own such items." Sarah thought appreciatively of Alice's forethought and said aloud to the walls, "Thanks Alice." She walked back downstairs feeling very warm indoors, dressed for outside weather.

She decided "I'll just wait outside on the porch swing for everyone else." and headed out the front door to wait on the wide porch swing, the yellow dog no where to be found. At the appointed time, Maria came out with Sam who was carrying a box of envelopes. Sarah sighed with apprehension "Those must be the letters" she thought to herself nervously. Cassi and Rosa were in tow puffy eyed and somber in their Sunday best. Once on the porch they all headed over together to get Lucas, who bunked in the bunkhouse with the other male work hands. Then they all got into a brick red Suburban and drove off up passed the barn towards the crest of a small hill in the far north east corner of the property where Sarah could see a small group of people standing.

Sarah picked Jo out even at a distance, standing stiffly with a gray felt Stetson hat topping a long black duster. Already there were a number of cars and trucks huddled up against the lower part of the hill and Sarah saw a small low fence encircling the top of the hill as they approached that she had not noticed before. A few minutes later the vehicle stopped and they all climbed out and walked the last several yards to the top of the ridge. There must have been close to thirty people gathered, Sarah noticed Sally's head sticking out of a burgundy jacket. She nodded a hello and Sally smiled reassuringly. Many of the work hands were there and a few other people Sarah didn't recognize at all. Sarah searched the faces to find Jo again and finally spotted her on the far side of the small circle of people looking withdrawn and haggard. There was a small circle of space between her and everyone else and Sarah realized with resigned sadness that it was very unlikely that the two of them would speak again before her flight that afternoon.

Lost in pain, Jo did not even look up from the small pile of dirt under which she knew her mother's remains were. Jo was completely unaware of the crowd that had gathered around her and the pile, only that pile of dirt existed for her. She had come out there early that morning and dug that small hole and buried the little cardboard box that the funeral home had given her, Alice adamantly refusing even an urn. "Such a small box underneath such a little pile of dirt." she had thought in a pain filled haze as she had smoothed the dirt into an even mound with her bare numb hands. She had removed her gloves wanting as little as possible between her mother's remains and herself and stuffed them in a pocket before starting the task.

Sarah noticed the dirt ground into Jo's blue jeaned knees as the wind whipped her long duster open and wondered at it. Jo looked like maybe she had been working already that morning. Sarah realized with a start that Jo was absently holding a small shovel in bare hands, bluish white with cold, and she knew instantly where the dirt on Jo's knees had come from.

She looked at the little naked pile of dirt in the middle of this crowd wondering why there were no flowers Sarah thought sadly to herself "Probably another demand from Alice," and tried to casually move around to be closer to Jo. "At least I might catch her eyes for a minute. I hope she knows that I have to go back to Houston. I'm not just leaving her, not abandoning her. I have to go," but Jo was in her own world.

Sam cleared his throat and began reading the page that Alice had written in a quiet voice as the wind tried to drown him out. Sarah heard bits and pieces of it through her tears and the sharp damp whipping wind. "I shouldn't have come to this." she thought miserably. When Sam finished there was silence, except for the wind that slid in between everyone, leaving each person alone with their thoughts for a while. Abruptly Sam broke into her thoughts when he started reading out names and people began to slowly get their envelopes and disperse. Both her and Jo's heads jerked up in unison when Sarah's name was called and their eyes grazed each other for an instant. Sarah's eyes full of tears from the service and the wind and Jo's so distant and filled with pain, that Sarah was not even sure that Jo recognized her. Then Sarah walked up to Sam on unsteady legs and got her envelope.

She immediately walked off by herself, down passed the cars, out of the reach of Sam's steady voice that continued to call out names, back towards the house and held her envelope in fingers that were quickly numbing from the cold wind. She would read it later she thought when she could see. Right now her eyes were so full of tears from the wind, Jo and Alice's death that she could hardly see were she was, going much less read anything as upsetting as words written by fingers that no longer existed.

Later, Sarah found herself lying on her back on the bed in her room, tears sliding from her eyes into her ears again as she came back to awareness. She didn't remember walking back to the house or going to her room. She didn't even know what time it was. Glancing at the clock beside the bed, she discovered that it was much later then she thought it should be. Realizing that her plane would be leaving sooner instead of later especially taking into account the drive in to town, she jumped up and began packing the last few things she still had out as quickly as she could. Sarah was a very methodical packer after many trips to many places and so she started in the bathroom quickly packing everything away in her luggage that lay open on the bed. In very short order she had everything packed, but for the life of her she could not locate her sketch pad, and though she searched high and low for the remaining time it was just no where to be found.

Finally out of time and with a desperate lump in the pit of her stomach, she headed for the door without the sketch pad. "That sketch pad is full of my deepest thoughts and feelings," she thought hoping that no one found it and that if they did, they would at least respect her privacy and return it to her unopened. But she knew that someone would, eventually find it, she hoped beyond hope that it would not be Jo. Nervously she wondered what the person who found it would think of all of those sketches of Jo, the pad was nearly full of them, and her abstracts of the anger, confusion, and sadness she felt. She thought of all of the raw emotion imprinted in those pages and sighed, "Can't be helped now, I have got to go or miss my flight," she pushed the button next to her door and Sam appeared "Sam," she said surprised, expecting Maria.

"Hi, Sarah, you ready to catch that plane?" he asked way ahead of her.

"Yes, I guess I am." she responded, her words full of reluctance and sadness as he grabbed up her luggage, giving her an understanding look and headed down the hall to the stairs. Sarah took a last look around her room, turned off the light and closed the door with a sad certainty that she would never return to this house again.

Chapter 11

Once settled in her business class seat, pleased with herself on the free upgrade she negotiated, Sarah thought back on her good bye. The hugs and smiles and wave of hands as she got into the Suburban with Sam and the promises from Maria to keep her informed about "things" and her certainty that this chance, this potential life with Jo was over before it had a chance to begin, all tugged at her already sad heart. She tried to think about how it could have possibly worked out any way, her art career in Houston, primarily, although she had begun to get some national recognition of late, and this ranch way out here in the middle of no where and then there was Jo's unwillingness to open up to her. Sarah sighed, "It could have all been worked out" she thought, "anything that felt this right could have been worked out. It would have taken some effort though." Sarah conceded "Maybe too much effort for Jo."

She sighed heavily and slowly turned her thoughts to Houston and the art opening at Barb's gallery. "Maybe I'll talk to Barb about going out and meeting some of her friends. Won't she just fall over with surprise," Sarah thought, although she suspected that Barb had her own thoughts about the reason that Sarah didn't relate to men well. She suspected that Barb wouldn't be overly surprised by her request after all. Then there was her mom. She shied away from dealing with that for the time being. "No reason to rush in until I'm sure." she said to herself, knowing in her heart that this would be a subject that they would have to talk about eventually. "Mom is not going to be happy about this." Sarah thought sadly, "She'll probably think that my artist friends had something to do with it somehow. She has never approved of my free style life anyway...just one more nail in my roadway to hell in mom's eyes," she sighed in frustration.

Finally her flight landed. Having no sketch pad to draw her time away with, had left her nothing to do but sit and think and when those wheels hit the ground in hot, humid Houston, she had a plan already developing on what she would do next. Sarah needed a plan right now to help her deal with the loss of Alice her mentor and guide for the last five years. Alice had been her bravery when it got tough, her forever optimistic cheering squad. And Jo, "Just forget her Sarah." she kept telling herself "Just forget her, accept the lesson and move on. At least she taught you a very valuable thing. She taught you that you have been looking for love in all the wrong people, men, and that is why you haven't found Mr. Right, because I need a Ms. Right. Right? Be thankful for that and move on, because she is never going to talk to you again probably. No not probably, she is never going to talk to you again. Admit it Sarah, no matter what Sally said you were just weekend entertainment for her or something." A wave of deep sadness washed the sand from under her feet and she could feel herself falling into the pit again. She got her luggage and hailed a cab and headed back to her little two bedroom apartment, now shock full of little post its notes from her long time friend and neighbor George about this and that, that had happened while she was gone.

Once home Sarah dumped her luggage on the couch and began reading her way through the apartment as she silently moved through her home. "Borrowed your milk", one said "figured it would go bad anyway" was scrawled on another directly underneath. "found this" was on another one on the counter with a big arrow pointing down to a small white shell button "don't know what it goes to though" was in small print along the side of that sticky note. Tabetha, Sarah's long term cat, stretched and wandered over to inspect her luggage, purposefully ignoring Sarah for the time being. "Fourteen years old and she still has an attitude." Sarah thought with amusement. "She's stuck with me longer then practically everyone else I know." she walked over noticing a few sticky notes that had been casually chewed up and batted around on the floor, and began saying her hello to her cat. Tabetha continued to ignore her for a little while longer for good measure, before settling into her lap for some petting and purring. Sarah remained in her only really comfortable chair, a large old leather chair full of cat marks she had found set out for the trash one morning, for a long time. Tabetha finally jumped down and wandered off to find other cat things to do, leaving Sarah sitting there deep in thought.

Finally, dark enough in the room that she had to turn the floor lamp next to the chair on to see, she decided it was high time she unpack, shower and eat a light meal before calling it a very long day and getting some rest. "Time enough in the morning to listen to the answering machine and check my email" she thought "and to organize myself back into my Houston life." After locating some crackers and cheese and getting her bags unpacked she took a quick shower in her tiny bathroom and slipped off to curl up in her comfortable bed. Although she wished for the softness of a feather bed she thought, "In the Houston heat it would probably make me sweat anyway."

Sarah awoke from dreams of green rolling Montana hills and crisp cool air blowing through her hair. Wise blue sparkling eyes watched her with loving approval as she stood on the edge of a high cliff, spread her wings and flew over the beautiful rugged land. Free at last. She felt herself soaring over the land higher and higher up into outer space. She looked down on the world from the moon. She blinked away the dream trying to separate the here and now from the powerful dream, absently reached for the sketch pad she kept by the bed and tried to capture the feeling of Alice's comforting love before it was gone. As the dream faded and she became more fully awake, she set the pad aside to the joy of Tabetha who had been waiting impatiently for her morning time taste of canned cat food by stomping over Sarah and under the pad as Sarah had worked.

Sarah petted Tabetha for a while and then climbed out of bed and checked her message machine. Making short notes to herself about a few of the messages, she mostly just listened to the short list of people calling just to see what she is up to, and a few remembered and wished her luck on her new opening and one call to let her know that they would be there. Then she made a few quick calls of her own and settled down to check her email. There blinking on the screen was an email from Alice, obviously written to her just before she had left to go up there. Sarah opened it cautiously. All it said was "can wait to see you! Alice" Sarah sighed and left the email in her in box to read again, unwilling to erase it just yet. There was one from her art agent suggesting that Sarah consider checking her email from someone else's computer every now and then while she was on vacation. A second email from her art agent asking why she hadn't read the first email she had sent her yet, a third saying never mind that they had just framed it the way they saw fit and that it was too late for her input anyway now, and that she was sorry to hear about Alice and for her not to be late to the opening. "Don't forget 6 p.m. sharp"

Sarah sighed, her mild annoyance at this energetic, friendly and pushy woman who found her all of the wonderful spaces to show her work and worked out all of the details for her, leaving Sarah her time to paint. It had been Alice's suggestion that she find an art agent. She thought back to before June's presence when she was trying to do it all. "It was just too much, absolutely overwhelming for me. June just does it all. Truly an incredible woman when you consider that she represents several other artists too, not just me." After reading through and deleting nearly two hundred and fifty emails, mostly junk mail that she deleted out of hand without reading, Sarah went into the kitchen and made some coffee and located a breakfast bar. She took her vitamins and headed into her studio, which was what would have been a second bedroom if she hadn't converted it.

Sarah remembered that big party she threw when she was ready to make room for a studio, sacrificing a lot of stuff, releasing it to her friends and what was left to resale shops in order to have the space for a studio. She remembered how hard it had been to let go of all of that stuff, but now she rejoiced in her studio. The smooth clean tables and her full size easel with rollers in the corner, "That easel sure was a hell of an expensive purchase, but worth every dime" she thought with pleasure.

Her gaze slid over the drying racks that now held four very dry canvases that she had been working on before she left. Everything was in it's place and she left closing the door behind her. "It was a good idea to leave the phone out of that room," she thought, aimlessly wondering around the rooms and straightening. She ran a few errands, dropped her dry cleaning, washed her dirty clothes, and cleaned up the kitchen to keep her mind off of Alice, Jo and her opening.

As the day wore on and she began to run out of things to do, she tried to catch a nap before the big opening. Sleep was impossible though so she wound up lying in bed and playing a silly cat game with Tabetha for a long time. It involved Sarah wiggling her feet up under Tabetha who would pretend to not notice until the last moment. Then Tabetha would roll over or pounce and 'kill' Sarah's feet with much rolling around on the bed and even occasionally falling off of the bed too.

Finally it was late enough that Sarah could get ready and go on down to the gallery, visit for a short time with Barb and Jodi and have it not look too suspiciously early. With one last wish me luck to Tabetha, who was sitting in the window and ignoring her in preparation for her departure, Sarah headed out to her little teal Corolla and set off for the gallery. Traffic was light and she was there in no time, highly unusual for Houston, "I must have slipped in between two rush hours somehow." she thought to herself sliding her car nimbly into a parking space near the gallery's front door. She unconsciously checked herself in her rearview mirror and curled a strand of her hair back behind her ear where she hoped it would stay.

Parking lots always had seemed like a fairly dangerous place to Sarah and she looked around getting her bearing and making sure that there was no one around her car before she unlocked the door and got out, locked her door and shut it all in one smooth motion and was off towards the gallery's door. She was smooth but not in a hurry, cautious but not particularly afraid. Comfortable in her dressy black sandals, black slacks and soft gray blouse, she had twisted her hair into a knot at the base of her head and pushed two chopsticks through it to hold it in place. The over all effect was simple and elegant. She rapped on the glass of the gallery door, knowing that Barb and Jodi would be there already doing last minute things and June's car was in the parking lot, so she had to be in there too. An indistinct form materialized on the other side of the frosted glass, she heard the bolt in the door slide and it opened a crack.

Barb's friendly face looked out all prepared to tell the early customer that it would be another hour or so before the opening started and that she was sorry for their wait, but one look at Sarah and her eyes changed expression and brightened "Oh, Sarah! Come on in, woman! Hey, you are early, that's great! You can look over our placement of your work and make sure we have everything right side up!" she joked as she opened the door wide and admitted Sarah into a powerful blast of air-conditioned cool.

"How is it possible that one minute outside down here is enough to glue any shirt to your body?" Sarah complained to anyone who would hear her.

"Oh. So we liked the cold Montana air did we?" asked Jodi with a sparkling glint in her eye as she glided gracefully up to Sarah and gave her a big long hug.

"That's not all I like about Montana." Sarah sighed looking downcast.

Everyone looked at each other in surprise and back to Sarah, but Barb was the one to ask "Sooo, what? You met Mr. Right up there but he was married or something?"

Sarah scowled, paused and then taking a deep breath decided she would just say it and replied as casually as she could "No, I met Ms. Right. But unfortunately she is Alice's daughter and right after we, uh, met... Alice, well, died and then I had to come back here, and I just know I'll never see her again, and I don't know what I'm going to do." Sarah stopped determined not to get upset right before her opening she took several quick breaths before continuing, "...so I was thinking that maybe I could go out with you and Jodi sometime and see if I can meet a Ms. Right here in Houston....sometime...." she glanced apprehensively around at Barb, Jodi and June who were all looking at her in stunned silence.

No one said anything, and Sarah's mask of casual "it's okay" began to slide a bit as tears glistened in the edges of her eyes. She blinked rapidly to make them go away and Barb said "Geez, Sarah... Who was this woman that stole your heart. I've never seen you so upset." and gave her a much gentler hug. Sarah quickly pulled away trying to regain her composure and knowing that she was on the verge of breaking down and sobbing, she just shook her head and she gasped "I'm just going to go to the rest room and freshen up for a minute." and dashed off to the back.

Barb, Jodi and June eyed each other for a minute silently. Finally June asked, "Well, do you think she's going to be up for this opening?"

Barb and Jodi looked at each other and then at June "Yes," they said in unison. Barb added with determination "Sarah is going to be just fine." and headed off into the back of the gallery too, leaving June and Jodi to finish up the last minute preparations.

Barb tapped lightly on the bathroom door "Hey, is there room for another person in there?" she queried.

"Sure" came Sarah's muffled reply from through the door.

Barb opened the door and walked in. She casually went over to the sink and began to wash her hands and asked, "So, are you excited about this opening like you usually are or what?" Then added "I know your friend died and you're still dealing with that, but that must have been some kind of a woman to knock your legs out from under you like this. You absolutely sure you are not going to see her again?"

Sarah, still sniffling, answered each question in the order asked "Yes I am excited about the opening, yes it was a big shock the way Alice didn't even tell me she was sick and then she died out of the blue as far as I was concerned, and no I am not absolutely sure I will not see her again....but I don't think she wants to see me again."

Barb was quiet for a while and then nodded "Well, me and Jodi would be glad to show you around the town and even introduce you to a few friends of ours who just happen to be single if you really figure it is over. However, if there is a chance that it is not over, I want you to say so now. Because you would break a heart if you started something with someone down here and then what's her name came calling and you went running off to Montana." Barb handed Sarah another tissue after she dried her hands.

Sarah considered her words for a time and answered, "Well, maybe I would like to just go out and make some new friends and think about all of this before I actually start dating. I mean, I don't even know how to go about this. I need some time to get used to this new understanding of who I am and what it all means to me."

Barb nodded her understanding and replied "You know Jodi has always been certain that you were barking up the wrong tree and that was why you just could not find someone that meant anything to you. I myself had my moments when I agreed with her and my moments when I did not, but we have always liked you buckets full and we will both be more then happy to talk with you about anything and show you around. However, right now you have an opening about to happen, and I need you to be your smooth happy, elegant self, okay?" Barb coaxed as she hugged Sarah briefly "So I'm going to leave you here to regroup and think about the opening and NOT about what's her face in Montana, for a while and expect to see you in a little bit. It is all about focus Sarah....and tonight your focus should be on yourself and your work and your opening..."

"Her name is Jo" Sarah yelled down the hallway at Barb's back only to get a vague wave and an unintelligible reply. "Jo" she said again out loud. She stood there for a moment and thought "Barb is right, it is all about focus and tonight I do have to focus on this opening, my paintings are on the walls for everyone to see. Beautifully framed and organized by June in a smooth motion from one expression to another, from one general color theme to another. I can not let these wonderful friends of mine down by being a silly sop tonight, right now." She straightened her shoulders and smoothed her

Jillian Carole

hair, tucking that loose strand behind her ear yet again. She washed her face and thought about all of the people she would get to meet tonight. Some faces she would know from previous openings, now that she was getting a small following, mostly women. She looked herself up and down and decided that she would do and headed back out into the front of the gallery to inspect the placement and framing of her work. The only change she made was to switch two paintings and their corresponding explanation card feeling that they worked better in a slightly different order now that she was seeing her work through newly opened eyes.

Chapter 12

Barb called about a week after the opening and invited Sarah to come along with her and Jodi "Yea, we're going out dancing at a local bar and it should be a lot of fun..." Sarah took a big breath and accepted and was now sitting in the back seat of a two door Honda shoulder to shoulder with a nice stranger named Sherl who had said maybe a total of three words to her including the initial 'hello.'

Sarah fidgeted nervously, trying to find some way to put her legs in the tiny back seat that did not involve having her knees poking Jodi in the back or touching this obviously shy woman next to her or sitting with her legs wide open either. "Okay, you two, no more of this blind dates with out prior notice for me." she thought with mild exasperation thinking back about ten minutes ago when she walked out and discovered that there were three people in Barb's small car not two. "Next time I meet you there." she continued mentally fussing to herself, "If I had known you were bringing me someone to meet I would have gotten some expert advice on what to wear from George."

"And it would probably have taken me ten times longer to decide on what to wear and it probably would not have been this." Sarah thought to her self and then sighed aloud in exasperation drawing an embarrassed, quizzical look from Sherl. She had finally settled on her camel colored dress slacks, a pair of low-heeled sandals and a sleeveless emerald colored, silk top, having no idea what to wear 'out.' She had immediately noticed that everyone else in the car was wearing nice jeans, boots and T-shirts. "I'll get you for this you two" she silently vowed, her shining emerald eyes green slits of nervous mischief.

Very early the next morning, when Sarah was finally home and lying in her full sized bed, she reflected on the evening. True, dinner was strained until the ice finally broke. Sarah was not sure what did it, probably because of the margaritas more then any one other factor. Then she and Sherl had begun getting to know each other and to relax a bit. The club had looked like any small club she had ever been to, dark and smoky, except that there were almost exclusively women in it, some in groups and some paired off alone in their own private world. Everyone seemed to be having a good time. The dancing was great fun, since there was no need to constantly defend from unwanted grabbing. Sherl was a really good dancer and in the end they had exchanged phone numbers and promised to go out dancing again. "Over all, the evening really was a lot of fun after all," Sarah thought to herself, "and once we got to the club there were other women dressed up a bit so I didn't feel so out of place."

But, innocently, her thoughts turned to the little club in Montana, for comparison, and then from there, with even less effort to Jo. "I wonder if Jo can dance. She has such a cats grace about her, I bet she's a fantastic dancer." Sarah thought imagining Jo taking her hand and the warmth of it on hers as they walked out onto the dance floor. Then there was Jo sliding her hand around to the small of her back, "maybe she would pull me in tight to her so our stomachs touched like some of those couples on the dance floor were dancing." Sarah thought closing her eyes and letting the night in Jo's arms unfold.

Before she knew it Jo's hands were running over her nude body and they were in Jo's huge bed again. Sarah gasped at the power of her imagination to pull up the memory of Jo's hands on her body and the heat that the two of them had shared that one night.

Shaking her head in frustration and misery at her inability to forget, she got up to go and get a glass of water and sit at the kitchen table for a while. Tabetha stretched and followed her into the kitchen hoping for a little tidbit of something or other, but settled for petting and behind the ear scritching as she paraded back and forth in front of Sarah on the kitchen table. "Surely I will be able to find someone else that makes me feel that alive. There has to be someone here in Houston right this minute that will set my soul on fire like that." she thought to herself "It's just a matter of finding them." she said out loud "I just know there is someone else for me," Sarah said with more conviction then she felt. "There just has to be," she whispered to the bright early morning sunlight. Tabetha purred a friendly 'I like you' and rubbed her nose on Sarah's cheek while Sarah gave up and let the tears fall again for her lost friend and for Jo.

The next morning Sarah turned the phone ringers off and walked into her studio feeling ready to work hard. She had been developing an idea for a series of paintings based on the emotions of her trip to Montana. "I'll use big canvases to capture the feeling of that big Montana sky," she thought. The knowledge of silence was a blessed relief. No one would be disturbing her today. Working in her "at home" sketch pad, a huge pad that enabled her to develop large sketches of paintings before she started on the huge canvases, she worked most of the day. Then about mid afternoon she took a break, jumped online and ordered eight large canvases to be delivered. "So much more convenient then trying to fit them in my car or tie them on top" Sarah thought with approval. "How about a little snackaroo, what do you say Tabetha?"

"Meow," Tabetha replied with interest.

"Then maybe check the mail and then see if anyone has called that I want to talk to?" Sarah continued.

"Meow, meow" Tabetha seemed to think of a possible alternative to going outside.

"How about it kitty kat? Sound like a worthy itinerary?" Sarah added.

"Meow" Tabetha answered unequivocally tail straight up for added emphasis.

Sarah continued to chat with her cat as she walked into the kitchen followed by quite paws and a few more 'meows' of approval when the snackaroo was delivered as promised.

After a quiet meal of tuna fish salad sandwich, shared of course, and iced mint green tea, Sarah returned to her studio, forgetting all about the mail and answering machine, her mind swirling through the Montana paintings and wishing she had been able to find her art pad before leaving. "Maybe I'll give Maria a call and see if she can find it for me. I just don't think those photos are going to be enough," but she shied away from the call because of the chance that Jo might be the one to answer. "Maybe later." she decided "When I'm to the point where I have to have it."

Late one night, several days later, Sarah abruptly decided she was ready to read Alice's note. She had saved it, unable to even open the envelope, but now she suddenly felt ready to read what Alice had written to her and folded and put in that thin legal sized envelope just for her to open. She carefully opened it and pulled out the one page typed letter.

My dearest Sarah,
You will never know just how much sunshine and joy your spark brought into my life. If you are reading this, it means that I am dead and probably didn't even get to tell you all of this myself. If I did, that is even better of course,

now you also have it in writing so you can read it when ever you start feeling unsure of yourself or your art. I love you and your work and think you are a wonderful, good-hearted woman. I want you to keep at your work for as long and as far as you want to go with it. I want you to go back to school and finish that degree that you always wanted. I want you to love yourself. I have a lot of wants for you because I care for you so much. I look at you and see so many of the things that I wished for in a daughter or daughter-in-law even, if that is the right term.

Please remember I love your special spark and believe in you, as you make your journey through life. The artist's way is not understood by most people, which can make life harder then it should have to be, but that does not make it wrong or unnecessary or silly. That is why I want you to just accept my gift and not get all weird about it Sarah. I have plenty, please understand.

Love always your devoted friend,
Alice

Tears rained down from Sarah's eyes blurring the words as she carefully folded the letter and put it away for safe-keeping. "daughter-in-law? She means Jo. Alice must have written this after we talked. Impossible, Oh Alice.....just impossible....." She cried herself to sleep that night.

Chapter 13

Jo showed up with out warning at the club one night, about to settle herself in to a long night of drinking. With raised eyebrows at the bad state she was in the bartender dug through his purse and found Sally's number and gave her a quick call from the back. "Hey, Sal, girl you need to get your butt up here and attend to your friend Jo, she's in bad shape from the look of her. I don't know if she has eaten in days...didn't her mother just die or something ...Hello?" hanging the phone back in the receiver he thought "Well, I guess that means she's either on her way or doesn't want to know about it."

Jo hunkered down over the bar and didn't say anything.

Knowing her favorite drink was Jack Daniel's over ice, the bartender waited to see if she would ask for it or not. Jo didn't say anything. So he moved on to other customers, leaving her alone, but keeping an eye on her. "I've never seen her like this before." he thought to himself as he busied himself with wiping off the bar top.

Very shortly Sally showed up, looking a bit worn out and more then a little bit concerned. Her concern deepened visibly when her eyes landed on Jo. "Damn, she looks really bad." she thought to herself as she made her way casually over to the bar "Hey friend." she said, softly resting her hand on Jo's shoulder. "I haven't seen you around lately. It's been about three weeks since I saw you last at your place, when we gathered for your mother's goodbye...I guess, right?" Sally paused but Jo made no reply so she continued "woman you just look like shit."

Jo turned her head and Sally could see the deep sadness in Jo's eyes "She left." was all she said.

Sally thought at first that Jo was talking about the fact that her mother had finally died, but almost immediately understood that this was about Sarah as much as her mother. "Ah," she said quietly "Yes, Sarah did go back to Houston, but I don't know if she actually left." Sally added, "I mean I think she left a part of herself here, and I think if you were to try to contact her she would probably come back up her to see you when she has time. You know she has a career of her own. She's an artist and that has got to take time and attention." Sally said in a soothing voice "She had an opening that she had to go to. It's not like an artist can have an opening and not go now is it Jo?" she asked hoping to pull Jo into talking some more.

Instead Jo just hung her head and rested her forehead on the top of the bar and repeated "She left," inside she was beating herself to a bloodied pulp over her mother's death and longing for Sarah at the same time. Hating herself for not saying something to her the night she lay on the dock or at the service for her mother or sometime or even leaving her a note like she had planned. "Why didn't I just ask her to wait for me, just a few days, surely she could have done that," she moaned to the floor, forehead still on the bar. "I went into her room to leave a note, but could not figure out what to say, wound up leaving without putting anything down on paper and worse I stole her sketch pad, Sally. I'm a fool," she rolled her head to the side and eyed her friend and said "Sally, I need help on this one. I give up. You still got that number you've been sticking under my nose for the last three years for that shrink? What's her name? I just can't take another step. I can't do it Sal."

Sally looked startled by the request but answered, "Sure, I've still got Amy's card, but it's at home." she knew Amy's number by heart, but lied to get Jo out of the bar and over to her house "Why, don't I take you home and we'll give her a call?"

Jo nodded silently and they walked out of the bar. Sally mouthed a silent "thank you" to the bartender and took Jo home. "I knew mom was going to go and was sort of ready for that," Jo said kicking a can in the parking lot, "but Sarah..." Jo trailed off into silence.

Sally wondered at the way Jo said Sarah's name, she could hear the love, sadness, confusion, the hope and fear, all in one word, "Wow, she's got it bad." Sally thought to herself. "I sure hope Sarah has it just as bad..."

Once there, Jo flopped down on Sally's futon and didn't move again until Amy showed up at the door looking mildly sleepy, like she had been woke up in the middle of the night, which she had.

Sally said "Jo, I want you to meet Amy, Amy this is Jo. I'll just let the two of you talk. Jo feel free to crash on the couch, lord knows you have enough times before. I'm heading back to bed." and with a nod from Amy and a concerned glance at the top of Jo's hat she headed off to the bedroom.

The next morning Sally awoke and found Jo and Amy still sitting and talking quietly on the couch. Both looked completely worn out. "Why don't the both of you take a break and have a little breakfast with me," she said as she walked into the room and headed for the kitchen. "Here, I'll mix up some orange juice, brew some coffee, and I even have the fixin's for pancakes, how about pancakes, Jo?"

Jo lifted her head and looked at Sally knowing that she needed to eat something, but having no appetite made it hard to want to "She's not going to take no for an answer Jo." she thought to herself and nodded 'yes' to her friend. "Thanks." she said out loud.

Amy smiled and replied, "That sounds great Sally. That sounds really great."

Sally didn't ask about what they had spent the night talking about. She didn't consider it her business and was not even very curious about it. She just wanted her friend Jo to be happy again like she had been before Melissa's accident. She had seen a glimmer of it that night Sarah rescued her from the bar too. "She just can't bottle any more up inside her with out breaking, not one more thing." she thought "Maybe I should email or call Sarah, see if she would consider coming up for another visit, so Jo would have something to hold onto. I'll ask Amy what she thinks, maybe that would be a bad thing to do."

During breakfast Sally tried to keep a little conversation going about the weather and ranching and non topics, but it was clear after a short time that Jo was not up for it and Amy was just too dog tired after being up all night to follow along any more, so without any rancor she stopped talking and they ate in a peaceful silence to the rhythm of knives and forks on plates. "At least she is eating now," she thought to herself watching Jo devour anything and everything that came near her plate.

After breakfast Amy suggested that Jo take a shower and then maybe try to get some rest, which Jo agreed to, quietly heading off down the hall, leaving Amy and Sally to talk. "It's a good thing you called me when you did and didn't wait until today. She was ready to talk and let it all hang out, I think if she had gotten some rest and food first, she would not have been so willing. I need you to take a day or two off of work. Can you do that? She needs company right now and I can't be here during my regularly scheduled appointments."

Sally nodded, "No problem, I have a bunch of time that I can take, a couple of days is no problem." she paused a moment and finally said "Did you two talk about Sarah at all? I know you can't tell me what the two of you talked about specifically, but I have been emailing Sarah back and forth, we've sort of become buddies and I think if I invite her to come back up, she would, she has it bad for Jo even though Jo doesn't know. I think the two of them are making each other miserable for no good reason other then pride. But what I need to know from you is, do you think it would it be a good idea or a bad idea?" she squared her clear blue eyes on Amy knowing that she would think it through and give her a straight forward answer.

Amy thought about it for a while and finally responded with an exasperated sigh "I didn't know that Sarah had any feelings for Jo at all, coming from her, it sounded like Sarah just sort of used her and when she was done, left off back where she came from," she looked Sally straight in the eyes "But you tell me that this Sarah, actually is head over heals for Jo still. After everything Jo has done to make this an impossible relationship?" Sally nodded and Amy thought some more "Well, hell." she cursed quietly "Jo could really use something good in her life right now, but it would have to be good, you understand me. If Sarah really is as indifferent as Jo describes her then this idea is a bad idea." Amy paused, eyeing Sally for a short time "However, this time I think you probably have the clearer eyesight." She finally nodded a yes "Okay, yes, sure drop her an email note or give her a call or what ever and see if she will come visit you, but don't mention how bad off Jo is, this is not going to be a little pity party, not if I can help it. Jo may not realize it yet, but she is not responsible for everything that happens around her. Primarily because, shit happens sometimes just because, with no good reason, but also because she is not as close to the center of the universe as she believes."

Sally looked surprised "Jo isn't self centered," she justified thinking about everything that had happened to her over the years "she's just preoccupied with that ranch, and I mean to lose Melissa like that and then her mother and to have Sarah leave without even talking to her..." Sally trailed off.

Amy shook her head, "I am not supposed to be discussing Jo with you, but hell, you know her better then she knows herself I think, and I could use some serious insight. Take for example the very fact that Sarah left without Jo even talking to her after her mother died... Why does she cut herself off so completely like that? I just don't get it. She told me about her cabin in the woods, and though that sounds like some kind of romantic big and strong thing to do...that is just not a healthy way to deal. If she has to go hide every time something upsetting happens, she's going to have a hell of a time running that ranch. How about when Sam goes or Maria, she has to look at this now and begin preparing. Parts of her emotional being are still running on a very young level." Amy sighed shaking her head. "I'm glad she has finally agreed to work with me. I think it will help her move into a healthier way of dealing with life."

Sally nodded "I'll go ahead and invite Sarah up then" she said quietly, glancing at the clock she picked up the phone and called her work to let them know that she would not be in for a few days, because she had come down cough, wheeze, with something bad, oh yea, a high fever too, just burning up. She hacked and coughed convincingly into the phone a few more times before hanging up and was immediately well again.

Amy who had been smothering a laugh let it roll out now while applauding her friend's performance and said "Sure sounds like you have done that before. I really thought you were sick for about a minute there."

Sally smiled and bowed, replying "I haven't done that for a long time and never for this reason. Usually that performance is reserved for long legged beauties," and laughed.

Chapter 14

Several days later the postman knocked loudly at Sarah's door and she answered it thinking that maybe the last shipment of canvases was in finally, five had arrived almost immediately but the last three were on back order. "Here's your mail, Sarah. I can't fit any more in your box, thought maybe you were out of town again or something, checked with George but he said no you were here...." he handed her a large pile of mail most of it junk from the looks of it.

"Ah, um, thanks." she answered smiling "It has just been so hot and by the time it is cool enough to get it, I forget and then another day happens" she shrugged uninterested in trying to explain how wrapped up she became when she was working on a project, and she was working. So she accepted the friendly offering and retreated into her cool kitchen again where she flipped through the envelopes, "bill, junk, junk, read later, junk, bill, what's this?" Sarah stared at the large cool white envelope postmarked Montana. "Looks like some kind of law firm or something. Awfully big envelope..." Sarah quietly opened it and found a terse note requesting her to return to Montana to sign some paperwork regarding Alice's estate and a first class round trip airplane ticket. Sarah was stunned. Tabetha rubbed her head on

Sarah's legs as she stood there unaware, her mind spinning, "What? What is this? WHAT?" She sat down not able to understand, "Go back? Go back to Montana? To Jo? To... Alice left me something in her estate? WHAT? I can't go back there. I can't. Jo will think I was after her mother's money after all. Oh, Alice what did you do? I can't go back. Not yet anyway. I'll just have to call them...." she looked on the letter head "these Kline, Smith and Huerenski people and tell them it's a mistake or something..." she glanced at the airline ticket noticing that they were first class tickets and then at the clock. "Too late today anyway, but tomorrow first thing I'll call them and get this all straightened out." she carefully put everything back in the envelope and set it on the table. "Well, I don't know if I want to check the answering machine Tabby, what do you think?"

"Meow." Tabetha replied still rubbing on Sarah's legs.

"Yea, okay I guess I should after all Sherl might have called. I sure do enjoy going out dancing with her," she walked over to the machine "Well, someone did call," she said to no one as she hit the play button. One very long message with a computer generated voice played out until her machine cut it off and then there was Sally's voice sounding a bit nervous "Um hey, this is Sally, I don't know if you'll remember me or not but I was thinking that it would be nice if you would come up and visit...um...you know stay with me and maybe... um...I don't know how to say this....Aw hell....come up and talk to Jo, she needs you right now Sarah......give me a call."

Sarah stared at the answering machine in disbelief. She hit save and replayed it two more times. "Jo? Need me? How in the world does Sally figure that? She wouldn't even talk to me when I was up there. How can she possibly need me?" She thought about the round trip air ticket sitting on the table and wondered at the coincidence, because that is what it had to be coincidence. "Well, at least if I do have to go up there for some crazy reason, I'll have a place to stay." she thought as she remembered how hard that futon couch had been. "Still it is a place, and Sally is a sweet woman, but I have only been home for…how long has it been now, three weeks, no nearly a month."

Chapter 15

Jo lay on her bed, having returned to the main house after two weeks of intense therapy and a good bit of coaxing from Sally. "It feel's so very empty all over again," she thought to herself sadly. She quietly pulled a sketch pad out from under her mattress where she had it hidden and slowly flipped through the pages. It was Sarah's.

Jo thought back to the moment when she had taken it. She had knocked on the door to Sarah's room and no one had answered. Really she had planned on leaving a note, something, but trying to explain had been impossible. In deep pain and frustrated at her inability to express her feelings, she had paced around the room for a long time caged in her fear that at any moment Sarah would come in the door and there she would be unable to explain herself. She passed that sketch pad again and again where it lay on the small table. Finally she threw herself into a chair and began flipping through it, as she tried to put her feelings into something she could write down. Initially she was just going to pull a piece of paper out of the back to write a note on, but there had been all of those pages and pages of pictures and as she flipped through she saw them. There in the pages had been sketch after sketch of her, there was Jo feeding the horses and there was Jo's face and there just a hand and there she was walking and without a second thought she had taken that book and fled tears running down her face in confused relief and fear not wanting to believe what she thought those sketches meant.

Now she slowly flipped through the worn pages and studied herself through Sarah's eyes. Realizing again, how much she had liked Sarah and how much Sarah had liked her. "But that is over now." she sighed to herself carefully closing the pad and then letting it slip onto the floor next to her bed "Over, over, over, I must move on. I must express my sadness and move on. I must release…" she lay in bed doing her breathing exercises and remembering Sarah's smooth body against her own and the release that she had felt when Sarah had made love to her. Never before had she let someone else take the reigns like that. Tears rolled down her face as she remembered her mother, Alice saying that she had "talked" with Sarah and the release of tension that had happened between mother and daughter as they had awkwardly gone to dinner that night, trying to walk a new pattern of acceptance with each other. "Release, Sarah, how can I release her? I love her, and I'm never going to see her again…I can't even figure out how to write her a letter. I can't even figure out how to return this silly wonderful sketch pad of hers."

Later that day as Maria cleaned Jo's bedroom, she noticed the sketch pad and remembered Sarah, as casually as she could, she flipped through it and her eyes got wide with sudden understanding. "Sarah, needs to come back. Everyone needs her to come back," she said to herself and leaving the sketch pad exactly where it had been she slipped away to find her husband Sam for a discussion and some planning.

Chapter 16

"I know I just got back June, and I am sorry, but the lawyers they say that I have to go up there to take care of this and that Alice stipulated specifically in the papers that I had to come up and handle it in person. Whatever 'it' is. Everyone is being very mysterious." Sarah sighed to her art agent, "but I will be back in a day or two no longer, just a quick pop up and back. Promise."

"Sarah, it's fine. Your last show did really well and this one is doing well too. You can do what ever makes you happy. You don't have any openings scheduled for at least two months. I thought you could use some down time so you can have time to contemplate and paint and so I can find a place to hang it. Go! Be happy." came June's cheerful reply over the phone.

"No, it's not like that. I'm just going to see Alice's lawyers, not Jo just the lawyers and I'm staying with Sally in town. I won't even be going out to that house......" Sarah said trying to sound convincing.

"Uhhu, sure, sure, what ever you say Sarah. Just go! And be happy! Speaking of going, I gotta go!" and with a click June was gone leaving Sarah unable to make any more excuses about the reason's for her trip back to Montana.

"George said the same thing! Why does everyone think I am going back to see Jo? I am only going to visit Sally and to sign those silly papers for Alice's lawyers." Sarah fumed as she waited for the taxi to show up to take her to the airport "I'll be there and back before anyone realizes that I am not in my studio." she paced back and forth "Where the hell is my taxi?" Tabetha took refuge under the table where she knew she would not get stepped on and talked to Sarah in friendly meows, agreeing with anything Sarah said. Sarah responded with "Uh no, not you too Tabetha, you traitor." she sighed again, knowing that the only person wrong about her motives for this trip was herself. She was hoping beyond hope to talk to Jo again "If only to have some kind of resolution, an end to the fairy book story, good or bad, but probably bad, but at least an end." she sighed heavily.

The trip to Montana was uneventful even though it was vastly more comfortable then her last trip and the food was better too. "So this is what first class is like." she thought to herself "amazing." She arrived at the small airport to no one. No red hat, no friendly blue sparkly eyes. No Jo either, much to her disappointment, although she would not admit to herself that she even remotely thought for an instant that Jo would be there to greet her. She only had her carry on luggage this time, so she walked over to the car rental place and rented a little car, "just so I can get around town more easily" she told herself, "not because I think I might go out to the house or anything like that." and headed over to Sally's house. Then halfway there she stopped realizing that Sally would not be there yet. She pulled into a parking lot and dug around until she found the letter from the lawyers firm and using a pay phone called their office. "Hello, this is Sarah Erickson. I'm in town and have a car and thought I would come on over if it would be okay?"

The receptionist put her on hold for a short time then came back on the phone and said in a hurried voice "How about Monday at

3:20? Would that be okay? They are booked solid right now, but have a little more time towards the beginning of next week."

"I guess that's fine, but I thought I just had to sign some papers for Alice." Sarah replied wondering why they had flown her up there if they weren't going to be able to see her for three days.

"Well, actually one of the partners is going to need to go over the rules governing the trust with you, so it's going to be a little more involved then that. It will probably take a couple of one hour sessions or so. Sometimes we tape the meetings for our clients so they can review between meetings and see if they have any questions."

Sarah sat in the sun in the car in the parking lot, stunned, "Trust? What trust? What are you talking about?"

"Alice set up a trust for you, Ms. Erickson. About two years ago, it was set up to provide you with a modest annual income with the only stipulation being that you go back to school and finish your degree. Alice felt very strongly about your education and set money aside specifically for that too, enough I believe for you to go full time until you get a Masters in Fine Arts. Hello?"

Sarah responded stunned "I'm here."

"Good! So we will see you Monday then to explain how this works?"

"Yes, Monday." Sarah replied.

"At 3:20 pm" she added

"Yes. 3:20" Sarah repeated in stunned acceptance.

"Wonderful" the receptionist said and promptly gave her directions to the office.

Sam winked at the receptionist and mouthed a silent "Thank you" to which the smiling woman shrugged indifferently and went back to work.

Sarah drove around town and then headed out towards the mountains. All afternoon she spent driving around the countryside aimlessly getting lost and then unlost and then lost again. She allowed the engine hum and scenery to calm her and in short order she was snapping reference photos all over the place. "I am so glad that I brought my camera again." she said aloud to no one "Last time everything green was so hesitant but now, wow! Flowers are everywhere and the green. This is a whole different type of green then I am used to." She took a deep breath and let the cool piney air fill her lungs to capacity and then slowly exhaled allowing herself to be in the moment and to enjoy everything about the day. She allowed the shock of what the receptionist had said to fade as she began to fully realize what Alice's Trust meant to her burgeoning career as an artist. Finally, as the afternoon passed into a blazing beautiful sunset, she remembered Sally. Knowing that she would probably be waiting on her, she headed back toward town. By supper she was settled in at Sally's, and they were laughing about the first night Sarah slept on the couch.

"You know" Sally said through chuckles, "That has been the most used piece of furniture that I own. More women have slept on that couch then in my bed by at least ten to one." she busted out laughing again.

Sarah quieted realizing that Jo had slept right where she was sitting, probably many times. She remembered her chiseled form and her skin marble like on the moonlit dock. Sarah sighed and Sally quieted and watched her quizzically.

"Oh, you have got it bad, don't you?" Sally shook her head, "Well, I'll tell you what, if you want we can go out and kick up our heels and maybe Jo will show up. Now she might not too, but she might. I could call her and see if she wants to meet me out if you like? I could see if she would like to meet you out."

Sarah went pale and she shook her head no "I..." she stammered, "I don't think she wants to see me," and she thought back to the last time they had spoken at the hospital.

Sally sighed in exasperation, "Woman! You are truly difficult. Do you want to see her or not?"

Sarah nodded a miserable yes "But I just know she hates me," she replied.

"Well then, let me give her a call. I promise not to mention that you will be coming okay?" Sally asked. Sarah nodded a silent 'yes' as Sally picked up the phone without even looking at her. "Hey is Jo around?" Sally asked someone on the other end of the phone. Then there was a long pause into which Sally whispered to Sarah "They've gone to find her, could take a..." she broke off as someone evidently picked up the line on the other end. "Hey, Jo. I was wondering if you wanted to meet me out tonight. Okay. Well how about in a coupla hours or so? Okay, see you there."

Sarah sat on the couch breathing and thinking, "Okay here we go. Remember, all you are looking for is closure so you can move on. Don't go in there expecting a happily ever after ending, or you will be really heart broken. They just don't happen." Aloud she said to Sally "Well, I have been going out dancing since the last time I was here. I even have a pair of new cowboy boots just for dancing and I even brought them along on the off chance that I might get asked to dance while I was here."

Sally started laughing but she seemed suddenly tense. As casually as she could she asked. "So are you dating anyone special down there in Houston? Have you found yourself a someone else?" Sally held her breath thinking, "Maybe this was a very bad idea."

"PFAH! I wish I could! You know, just find someone, anyone that could wipe Jo out of my mind. Here I have been gone nearly a month and still...." her voice trailed off into an unhappy silence.

Sally shifted from foot to foot, "Nope, not another woman problem after all. These two have to get together, they'll just go slowly crazy if they don't." she thought greatly relieved. "Oh well," she said aloud trying to sound casual, "Maybe I'll sweep you off of your feet on the dance floor and you'll forget all about Jo." and she started chuckling and ducked into the bathroom to get ready.

As far as Sarah could tell getting ready meant, changing into clean jeans and a shirt, and brushing your teeth and hair. Sometimes a woman would have on a nice smelling cologne or perfume. Occasionally a woman would have on a dress and heels, but usually they were coming from work and didn't have time to change or something like that. Comfort seemed to be a high priority. She thought about this while she changed into a clean pair of black jeans her one pair of boots and a teal silk blouse that she bought brand new at a real store at the mall. Unable to curb her need to wear a little bit of makeup she brushed her teeth and hair and then put on a little blush and freshened her eye makeup up a bit. "No lipstick though." she thought to herself as she remembered Jo pulling her down into her lap and Jo's lips covering her mouth in that mind numbingly soft kiss that lasted all night.

Sally cleared her throat and Sarah jumped, much to Sally's amusement. Sally said, "Now, what could you have been thinking about to make you jump that high. You sure were far away, those eyes of yours told on you." Sally smiled a friendly smile at Sarah and said "ready?" Not giving Sarah a chance to answer any of the questions asked, Sally swung around and headed out.

Sarah grabbed her ID and some money and followed Sally out the door, having learned that purses were hard to keep track of at clubs if you wanted to dance and Sarah wanted very much to dance the night away.

"Wow, there are a lot of people here for a Friday night." Sarah said. "I'm surprised that they are even open. Most of the clubs in Houston are pretty empty on Friday until pretty late."

Sally said, "Yea, it's our little way of doing the Gay Pride thing." she noticed Sarah's questioning looking and went on to elaborate, "A lot of gay and lesbian communities celebrate Gay Pride. It's a celebration of who we, as a community, are and how far we have come. Really pretty fun. This week there has been stuff all week going on, even a small parade, made it from the bookstore to the bar."

"Well, that sounds fun. I wonder if Houston has anything like that." Sarah said mostly to herself. Then she remembered Barb mentioning a night parade with lit floats and answered her own question "Hey, we do have something like that in Houston. One of my friends was telling me all about it. How it was a night parade with lit floats and everything! Imagine." she smiled at Sally proud to have remembered something interesting for her friend. "Maybe you can come and visit me next year and we'll go to the Houston Gay Pride celebration. That would be fun."

Sally glanced at Sarah concern once again reflecting in her eyes. "I sure hope I am making the right decision by getting these two together again." she thought to herself. "It's just got to be right. I just know this is the right thing to do." Sally smiled at Sarah and replied "Well, we'll just have to see where we are in a year now won't we." and with that they went in.

There were at least ten couples on the dance floor and instead of the jukebox music there was a three-person band in the corner playing country songs with modified words. Everyone seemed to be having a great time. Sarah was immediately happier "even if Jo doesn't come tonight I'm going to have a good time." she vowed to herself. "Sally," she said turning to her friend "do you dance? Because I do."

Sally smiled and nodded a sure and they headed out onto the small dance floor to have a try. Before long they were both talking over the music and laughing as they danced across the floor.

Sarah was keeping an eye out for Jo and so was Sally. Sarah kept scooting in close so she could here Sally's stories and Sally kept politely backing up to keep a little space between them. She kept thinking "If Jo comes in and we are dancing too close she's gonna flip. No if ands or buts about it, she will be out of here before we even get a chance to explain." Aloud to Sarah she suggested that they get a drink hoping to get her over by the bar before Jo got there.

Sarah said "Oh, come on one more dance and then I'll gladly head to the bar for a drink."

Sally said, "Oh all right one more but then these legs have got to rest," and to herself she thought "and wouldn't you know it would be a slow one. great. Please Jo just be late this once." but she knew that would be asking a lot.

The dance ended and Sally breathed a sigh of relief, "No Jo yet." she thought to herself as they headed off to the bar, but she was mistaken.

Jo was there leaning on the bar as if she had been there all evening or maybe just materialized in that very spot. She had on a pair of roper boots, Levi button fly jeans, white T-shirt and a straw Stetson. She was quietly looking at Sarah from under her hat brim, her eyes narrow slits of molten fire. "How can she be so unbelievably beautiful and so unbelievably cruel at the same time? Coming to town to visit with Sally and not even tell me. They are probably a couple from the way they are dancing so close." she thought to herself as she watched them dance. "Could she look any happier or more beautiful?" she continued her anger growing even as her knees shook at the sight of Sarah with her hair down and swinging heavy against her silk blouse each time they turned. Jo leaned harder against the bar trying to look casual as she remembered the coolness of Sarah's silk robe when she had slid it off of her shoulders before they had made love, memories of Sarah's silky body flooding in on her.

When Sarah and Sally finally left the dance floor Jo looked quickly down at her drink trying to feign indifference, but she couldn't leave her eyes there, she had to see Sarah, she had to drink her in. Jo watched the graceful smooth way Sarah walked and her stomach tightened even as her anger rose. Sarah saw Jo before Sally did and the sight of her and those eyes stopped her in her tracks and took her breath away. Quietly cursing herself for her inability to control the way she reacted to Jo, and nearly falling down on her way off of the dance floor, she silently grabbed Sally's arm for support. Sally felt Sarah grab her arm and spotted Jo almost at the same time. Sally knew instantly from Jo's eyes there was going to be hell to pay for that slow dance with Sarah.

Joined by forces that neither of them seemed able to could control, Sarah and Jo were unable or unwilling to look away from each other. Sarah felt the anger and fire in Jo's eyes as if she had been slapped across the face, "I should not have come!" she abruptly said aloud "This was a terrible mistake!" She pulled away from Sally furious with herself for hurting Jo. Sarah ran for the door, Sally following close on her heals.

"Sarah" Sally called after her "Sarah where are you going? Come back here." but Sarah, tears running down her face was out the door. "Sarah, Sarah stop." Sally called after her once out of the club. "Wait for me. Come on woman. Wait up."

Sarah slowed and finally stopped near Sally's car, "Oh Sally what have I done? I should never have come up here." she moaned tears running freely down her face.

Sally caught up with her and said, "What are you talking about?"

"You saw her. You saw Jo. She was so mad and hurt and it's my fault, I should never have come up here. I just knew she hated me. I knew it."

Sally patted Sarah awkwardly on the shoulder. She saw Jo coming out of the club and carefully positioned herself to block Sarah's view, hoping that she would speak her mind and Jo would hear it. Sally knew Jo would be heading over to them with murder on her mind. She raised her voice a little hoping Jo would hear what she had to say. "Oh, now Sarah, I don't think Jo hates you. In fact I suspect that she really likes you a lot."

Jo did hear and slowed her pace and then came to a stop behind Sally, listening, holding her breath and waiting on Sarah's answer, confusion washing over her. "Why in the world would she think I hate her, I love her," Jo thought desperately, "I just do not understand."

Sarah, still sniffling sighed, "It's no use Sally. She hates me. You saw her eyes. She hates me. I should never have even thought for a moment that there was any hope we could ever work it out. I should have never even come up here, but I just can't get her out of my mind. I should have let it all be in the past instead of hurting her all over again by trying to see her." Sarah began crying again. Deep sobs of a broken heart echoed around the empty parking lot. "Oh what am I going to do Sally? The woman I love hates me because she thinks I was after her mother's money. I didn't even know. I didn't even know."

Jo listened to Sarah's heart breaking. Then she quietly moved Sally out of the way and gave her a you-need-to-go-somewhere-else look. Sally nodded, slipping away back into the bar. Jo stood like a statue silent in front of Sarah. Sarah, oblivious to the switch, turned from where she had been leaning on the car and leaned forward, reaching for Sally's warm comfort. Expecting to find Sally's soft round body to hold onto, Sarah instead found a firm muscular frame in front of her. Disoriented, she tried to push away only to feel arms of velvet wrapped steel circle her waist and pull her fiercely close. Lifting her head up Sarah blinked trying to clear her vision "Jo" Sarah gasped catching the side of Jo's face in the light of the street lamp, she tried unsuccessfully to push a wedge of space between herself and Jo. Sarah could see a muscle twitching on the side of her face and thinking that Jo was angry with her still Sarah dropped her head in deep frustration. Jo silently lifted Sarah's chin with one of her strong hands forcing Sarah to look into the melting softness of her eyes. Sarah said, "Oh Jo, I'm sorry. I know now I shouldn't have come. I didn't mean to hurt you, Jo. I...I love you." Sarah burst into tears again and Jo released her chin and pulled Sarah into her. Sarah sobbed into Jo's shoulder and thought, "there I've said it at least. Now it's up to her."

Jo silently stroked Sarah's soft hair and breathed in the smell of her. It felt so right having Sarah in her arms again, even if she was crying. Then Jo spoke in a quiet, firm voice "Sarah," she almost whispered it. "Sarah, I need you. Sarah, look at me." she commanded in a firmer voice. She slid one of her hands up to cup Sarah's tear streaked face forcing Sarah's eyes to meet hers again.

Frightened that Jo's eyes might be filled with anger, Sarah steeled herself and opened her eyes. Instead of the liquid fiery anger she expected she found two pools of agonizingly soft hope looking down at her. She felt the steel grip around her waist loosen to a firm pressure, "Sarah, I love you too, and I'm the one that owes you an apology. I should have never let you leave without talking to you and letting you know how I felt. But I was too wrapped up in myself to see how much I was hurting you. I'm sorry, Sarah. Please...forgive me." Jo stopped and watched Sarah silently.

Sarah slid her arms around Jo's neck. She silently pulled Joe's mouth down to hers in reply, their lips meeting in mutual soft surrender. Slowly Jo's hands slid over Sarah's back and hips as they kissed "Oh, I can't get enough of this woman," she thought vaguely, enjoying the feel of Sarah's firm body against her own. Already Sarah could feel the fire building between them. She thought "One look and I'm hers...one kiss and..."

Jo lifted her head and breathing shallowly she looked into Sarah's bright eyes and shook her head "One kiss and I can't think about anything except taking you home and keeping you there forever, Sarah. What kind of spell have you cast on me?"

Sarah could feel the fire too "Me, cast a spell on you?" She breathed in delight at Jo's admission, "I'm the one that came back up here from Houston just to see you, not the lawyers, not really." pausing to look at Jo, she suddenly realized that Jo had known about the trust all along "You knew about that trust all along didn't you Jo?" she asked.

Jo looked into her eyes and then away, ashamed that she had ever thought that Sarah was after her mother's money, she sighed, "Yes, I even argued with mother about it, thought it was a bad idea to just give you all of that money, I'm the one that had it set up so you would have to spend it on college and living expenses only..." she sighed. "But that was before, before I met you, before I fell in love with you, just before." Jo pulled Sarah against her harder and kissed her again.

Sarah pulled away finally and shook her head. "How in the world are we going to make this work? My life is in Houston. Yours is up here."

Jo's grip on Sarah tightened as she responded with a fierceness that surprised herself "We'll just have to make it work, Sarah. We have to make it work."

Sarah was silent for a while, she leaned fully against Jo "It feels so right," she thought as she absently drew a small circle around and around on Jo's shoulder, knowing that Jo was right, "It's just got to work out." she thought.

Jo finally reached up and caught Sarah's hand, unable to think with her making little circles, and held it still. Then she silently pulled Sarah's hand up to her mouth and began kissing Sarah's fingers. Then Jo moved to the palm of her hand until Sarah's knees began to get weak. Jo's fierce hold around her waist kept Sarah upright throughout her gentle, sensual inspection of her hand. Sarah gasped when Jo's hand released her own, only to slide down the front of her shirt to cup one of her breasts. "Jo we are in a parking lot."

Sarah said quietly moaning in pleasure as one of Jo's fingers began to slide gentle circles around her nipple.

Jo's fiery eyes lifted from Sarah's face and she surveyed the parking lot in a single sweep. Silently, she moved her hand and loosened her grip on Sarah's waist and said "I'm sorry. I guess I forgot where I was. You do that to me, Sarah. You make me forget…everything." Again she looked around then released Sarah and lightly took her hand "Let's go back inside for a while, what do you say Sarah? Would you like to spend some time with me this evening?" Sarah smiled and nodded a 'yes' and together they and headed back into the bar hand in hand.

Once inside the bar Jo asked, "Would you dance with me?" seeing Sarah's reluctance she added "You danced with Sally, dance with me, Sarah." Jo's fiery eyes threatened to cloud up with jealousy.

Sarah got a strange look on her face and agreed to a dance "Okay, but don't hold me too tight, Jo. I don't know if I'll be able to stand up much less dance with you."

Jo laughed aloud, suddenly understanding Sarah's hesitation. "Yea, me too, but that's okay, Sarah. We'll just hold on to each other and do the best we can. What do you say?"

Sarah smiled and said "Okay, Jo." and so the two of them walked out onto the dance floor, found the beat together and began to dance.

Sally watched the room of people from her place against the bar and noticed that most eyes were on Jo and Sarah. "It has been a long time since Jo has danced with anyone." Sally thought to herself happily. "It's about time she found someone to dance with again."

Printed in the United States
108537LV00008B/7/A